TAMING JENNA

Sequel to Saving Grace

Stacey Espino

MENAGE AMOUR

Siren Publishing, Inc.
www.SirenPublishing.com

A SIREN PUBLISHING BOOK
IMPRINT: Ménage Amour

TAMING JENNA
Copyright © 2011 by Stacey Espino

ISBN-10: 1-61034-642-4
ISBN-13: 978-1-61034-642-9

First Printing: May 2011

Cover design by Jinger Heaston
All cover art and logo copyright © 2011 by Siren Publishing, Inc.

Printed in the U.S.A.

PUBLISHER
Siren Publishing, Inc.
www.SirenPublishing.com

DEDICATION

To my fellow Western authors on the Wild and Wicked Cowboys blog. There's just something special about a cowboy ;)

TAMING JENNA

Sequel to Saving Grace

STACEY ESPINO
Copyright © 2011

Chapter One

"The best day of your life is the one on which you decide your life is your own. No apologies or excuses. No one to lean on, rely on, or blame. The gift is yours—it is an amazing journey—and you alone are responsible for the quality of it. This is the day your life really begins."—Bob Moawad

Jenna supervised the cattle run from a distant hill, giving her a full view of the roundup. Her horse snorted and stomped, eager to join in the melee below, but she held him steady. She savored this time of morning when the new sun slowly lit up the land, changing the dark sky from navy to a robin's-egg blue. The dew-covered hay fields behind her smelled sweet and earthy. At this point in her life she could honestly say she was satisfied with her lot. She had a simplistic life doing what she loved. Her boss, Mr. Wagner, was a good and honest man. He paid her well, provided food and shelter, and most importantly, he kept her secret. The cowboys on the Wagner Ranch respected her and didn't give her a lick of trouble.

Would this life always be enough? Would there ever come a time when she craved more? Jenna scoffed at her own thoughts and pressed her heels against the horse's sides. Quiet reflection only served its purpose for so long. After that it just pissed her off.

She galloped at full speed, savoring the wind on her face and the rhythm of the horse's hooves on the hard-packed earth. The powerful beat tore through her body, completing her, vanquishing any misgivings she had about her future. Her skills in the saddle surpassed most of the hard-core cowboys working the ranch, and she loved every second of it. She sailed past Conner, a blur as she raced to the center of the roundup. Trevor and Bryce were leading this party. Jenna only showed up to help train a couple greenhorns. Mr. Wagner trusted her to be firm, but fair, and she'd never let him down.

"Jenna, keep track of your boys! They don't know shit." Trevor had to shout over the roar of the stampede. Her trainees were an embarrassment, but getting hired hands to spend the busy season on the ranch became more and more difficult, regardless of the paycheck. The kids these days were moving away from farming and moving to the cities to go to fancy universities. She'd never choose modern conveniences over the open land, but it seemed she was a minority.

"I'll deal with them my way. Get the cattle moving, foreman!" Jenna knew about everything that happened on the ranch. Whatever Wagner wanted done, she'd make sure it was done to his satisfaction.

"Yes, ma'am." Trevor waved his tan cowboy hat in a circle above his head and whistled. The crew followed his lead, and they continued to the east paddock, where they'd begin a weeklong branding of the new stock.

Jenna had known Trevor since she moved onto the Wagner Ranch six years earlier. He'd matured over the years, now a ruggedly good-looking cowboy with a sexual appetite to rival most of the men that passed through each season. She knew all about his kinky stories, even heard about them firsthand around the bonfire time and time again. To the men on the ranch, Jenna was just another one of the guys. That's the way she wanted it. The way it had to be.

She whacked the rump of Steve's chestnut gelding as she sailed past, signaling him to follow. Her new boys had had enough for one day. If she let them *help* any more with the roundup, the regular guys would have her by the proverbial balls tonight at dinner.

Back at the main barn, she dismounted before coming to a full stop, landing solidly on her prized cowboy boots. Mr. Wagner bought them for her twentieth birthday, and anything from him held a dear place in her heart. After gathering her rifle and belongings from her saddlebag, she led her horse to the water trough. She loosened his girth strap, planning to come and unsaddle him with her two-man trainee crew. They still hadn't arrived and should have been right behind her. This was more like babysitting than training. The two hired hands wanted a free ride, and she planned to show them that nobody screwed around with Mr. Wagner…or her.

A few minutes later Steve and Tanner showed up in the yard, laughing, without a care in the world. She was waiting, leaning against the side of the barn with one leg bent up. Today she donned her rifle because she planned to put the fear of God in these two jokers. "When I tell you to follow, I expect you to be right on my ass." With her rifle resting over her shoulder, she circled the two riders. She may be barely over five feet with a small frame, but she could outshoot or outride any of the men on the ranch, and they knew it. These boys would learn that in a hurry. They'd understand that she didn't offer second chances or do sympathy.

Steve had a shaggy mop of brown hair which seemed to be popular with the men these days. Tanner's hair was darker, but neatly kept. Although they were both tall, they hadn't filled out their frames yet. Not yet men in her opinion—not like the crew that lived in the trailers out back. Conner would eat them for breakfast if she wasn't watching them every hour.

They each looked at her, then each other, with condescending smirks. If they saw her as the weaker sex, they had a lot to learn. Once at the horses' rears, Jenna emptied a shot from her rifle into the air, the explosion of sound deafening. Both horses reared up and dumped their riders onto the mud and hay-littered yard by her feet. When they looked up at her with dazed eyes, she smiled.

* * * *

"Looks like Jenna's teaching the new guys a lesson," said Trevor. He chuckled when the distant shot echoed throughout the property, and he wished he had been there to witness Jenna's brand of justice. A few months earlier she'd shot Grace's ex-husband dead on the spot. The police investigation deemed it as self-defense because that bastard was off his rocker, but the regular cowboys still gave her a wide berth of space after the incident—wider than they usually did, anyway. Trevor rarely messed with her unless he was teasing. She was Wagner's treasure, so only a fool would get on her bad side. Besides, no matter how gorgeous the girl was, she was off-limits. Why did all the best women have to be married, nuts, or gay? If she'd been into guys, he had no doubt that he'd already know her luscious body intimately. Watching those curves day in, day out gave him blue balls when he barely had time to take leave into town for a quick fuck.

"How long you think they'll last with her as their teacher?" asked Conner.

"Normally, not a day, but she's been going easy on them. Wagner needs the new staff, so the pressure's on to shape them up rather than scare them off."

"Sounds like she's trying *real* hard."

"If my memory serves me, you were at the receiving end of her shotgun once upon a time." The whole ranch heard about Conner's temporary hearing loss from the shot that came a few inches from his head, tearing through the side of the barn. It taught him and all the other cowboys to keep their hands to themselves when it came to Jenna. Unfortunately for Trevor, dominant women rang his bell.

Trevor had been tense lately. Things weren't quite normal with all the wedding preparations going on for Wagner's only son, Scott, and Grace. They were having an outdoor wedding, and the planners never seemed to stop coming and going. It was all a pointless waste of money in his opinion, but Mr. Wagner wanted to go all out for the event. The whole thing forced Trevor to think about his own life, his own future. He was still young, but getting older each day. He supposed he'd need to settle down sooner or later, but the idea didn't comfort him, and he hadn't found a woman worth keeping. Working at the Wagner ranch gave him purpose. Living the single life and not having to answer to anybody suited him.

He'd admit to reevaluating his life after his time with Grace. She forced him to think about a future with one woman, only she wasn't the one for him. The sex had been great, and she was a sweet girl, but there was no spark between them. As much as he hated to admit it, Scott and Grace were perfect together. He wished them well, but couldn't help but feel sorry for himself, even though he should be the lucky one, not getting tied down.

They spent the next hour rounding up the new herd into the holding paddock. They'd keep them penned until the branding. His job was an excellent distraction for wayward thoughts. He loved getting dirty—the dust and sweat, his muscles aching after a hard day's work. This was a man's job, and there wasn't a prouder cowboy than him.

Once he cooled off his horse and set the gelding to graze, he carried his saddle to the tack room. The quiet inside the barn was deafening after running with the cattle. Only his heavy footfalls on the hay-littered concrete, and leather chaps brushing together, broke the hush. He placed his saddle on the saddle horse and then took off his cowboy hat, giving it a few good whacks on his thighs to remove the dust.

"Finished for the day?" asked Jenna. She leaned against the opening of the tack room sipping a can of Coke. It wasn't even lunch, so she had to be messing with him.

"You know I'm never finished. I've got a shitload to do and deliveries to make." He brushed past her into the center of the large barn. "You scare those greenhorns off?"

"No, they're washing up for lunch. You should get your ass inside before Pete throws a fit. You know he hates warming up your plate." Jenna walked to the open bay doors and stopped. He settled beside her, following her gaze. Out back, behind Wagner's house, hired workers were setting up large white tents for the wedding. It looked like a fucking circus. Only a few more days and it would all be over with. Trevor couldn't wait for things to get back to normal.

"Can you imagine spending all that money on one day?" he said.

"You know how much he loves Scott. I bet he'll do the same for you whenever you get hitched." She smirked.

"That'll be the day."

Before turning away from the sight, she took a cleansing breath, as if returning from a daydream. Her gentle reflection vanished in a heartbeat. "By the way, I want that front yard free of your pickup trucks starting today. Park them around back." The little firecracker was bossy as hell. If things were different, he'd love to bend her over his knee for a spanking.

"What on earth for?"

"Wedding guests. Wagner's expecting a load of guests today and tomorrow. If he wants the front yard clear, it'll be clear," she said, leaving no room for arguments.

He dipped his cowboy hat. "Yes, ma'am. Want me to wipe your ass, too?"

She rolled her eyes and gave him a healthy shove before heading back to the house.

He watched her go, her blue jeans hugging her curvy ass. His sexual attraction to her felt foreign because she was essentially one of the guys. You didn't get a hard-on looking at a buddy, but even though Jenna was into women, he couldn't help but appreciate her appearance. Blonde, blue-eyed, with a body to die for. He kept those impure thoughts to himself. Compliments earned cowboys a sharp kick in the balls when it came to Jenna. She hated anything remotely feminine and saw sensitivity as a weakness. The only time he ever saw her acting tenderly toward another person, besides Mr. Wagner, was when Grace stayed at the ranch for a month. The two women bonded, and she protected Grace like a mother hen. A lot of good that did, considering what Trevor and the other farmhands did with Grace when Jenna wasn't around. If only she knew, she'd skin him alive.

* * * *

After lunch, the guests started to arrive. Jenna glanced out the window to ensure Trevor had moved the trucks like she'd asked. They were gone. Good thing for him because she was in no mood for incompetence. She had enough of that from her trainees. Everything had to be perfect for the wedding. She loved Mr. Wagner like a father, and Grace deserved a special day. Although she never shared anything too personal about herself with the other woman, they enjoyed each other's company. That was as close to friendship as Jenna dared to get.

She rushed around the living room making last-minute adjustments. The place was tidy as a pin thanks to Pete's help. They had scrubbed the kitchen from top to bottom together the day before. She'd even emptied the fireplace of ash and cleaned the flue. Now it was time to receive guests. Jenna would play the hostess, anything to ease Mr. Wagner's burden.

"Jenna, is Scarlett's room ready? I just saw her car pull up out front." Mr. Wagner tucked the tail end of his shirt into his jeans. He had aged so well over the years. His body was lean and fit, his hair more pepper than salt.

"Everything's all set," she assured. Although the house was a modest bungalow, it had plenty of extra room considering Wagner lived alone now.

"You make sure them boys don't come in for dinner swearing up a storm. Scarlett has children, and they don't need their ears burning."

"Not a problem, Mr. Wagner. They'll be as good as gold." She could handle the rowdy crew of cowboys. If they dared to embarrass her or Mr. Wagner, they'd pay dearly.

He smirked and pulled her against his side for a hug. "You're a good girl. What would I do without you, darlin'?" After a kiss atop the head, he meandered to the door to greet his guests.

Amazing how one touch, a few words, could reinforce her complete and utter devotion to the man. He was the father she should have had.

Jenna stood to the side, hoping to blend into the background, but be available should Mr. Wagner need her for anything. If Ms. Scarlett had children, Jenna may be needed to keep an eye on them. She didn't know too much about the guests. They were all friends and family of Mr. and Mrs. Wagner's, but she'd only met a few in the past. Scarlett was a childhood friend of his and had known Scott when he was just a boy. Jenna expected a big reunion with plenty of laughing and sharing of old memories. God knows her boss deserved some good times. She'd watched his marriage deteriorate over the years and hated seeing him alone for the past year. Although he took life one day at a time with a positive attitude, he rarely left the ranch to visit friends during the past couple weeks. He buried himself in work around the farm and lost his carefree edge.

She knew Mr. Wagner was stressed about seeing his ex-wife. His ex was coming up from the city for their son's wedding, and then planned to leave the same day. If she could personally erase his heartache, she'd do it in a second.

"Scarlett!" Mr. Wagner greeted. "Look how lovely you are. You haven't changed a bit." He hugged the woman. She looked to be around his age, in her early fifties.

"Still generous with the flattery, I see. It's been over a decade, Wayne. I'm not a young woman any longer." Bryce came in behind her with two matching suitcases. Scarlett screamed money. From the way she moved to her designer purse and expensive hairstyle—she was a woman with class. Jenna wondered if she was as cold and snobby as Mrs. Wagner. Sometimes money had a way of souring a personality.

"You're a breath of fresh air." He kissed her knuckles. Such an old-school cowboy. "Now where're the children at?"

"Wayne. They're not children. Brittany's twenty-one and Brad's twenty-three. I told you, it's been a long time." She smiled and cupped his cheek with a well-manicured hand. "I've missed you."

There was a pause, as if time stood still for moment. Mr. Wagner definitely had feelings for their houseguest. Ms. Scarlett was a widower, but Jenna hadn't deemed her worthy of her boss yet. "In their twenties? I'll be. They're nearly as old as my Jenna."

Jenna straightened up upon hearing her name. Then she thought better and slouched her shoulders forward to disguise her too-large chest. Being a cowgirl with DD breasts was truly a curse. Some days she wished she'd wake up and discover she'd shrunk down to a respectable B cup like Grace, but every morning her burden remained.

"Jenna?" Scarlett took a step back. "I thought Scott was your only child."

"Of course. You know about the accident." After a rodeo disaster in his youth, Mr. Wagner could no longer have children. Lucky for him, his wife had been pregnant with Scott, or he'd never have known the joys of fatherhood. "Jenna works for me, but she's the closest thing I have to a daughter." He motioned her forward with a wave of his flannel-covered arm. She stepped into his reach. "As a matter of fact, anything you need, she'll be sure to get it for you."

"Yes, ma'am. I have all your rooms ready. Would you like to settle in?"

"Certainly." She smiled warmly, which pulled down Jenna's hackles. "Bryce, dear, did you see where my children disappeared to?"

"They were right behind me, Ms. Scarlett." Bryce turned around and was nearly run over by the two children in question. However, "children" wouldn't be the best description. Brittany was a beauty, taller than Jenna, with a lean figure. Her hair was reddish-brown like her mother's, her eyes an exotic green. It was a shame that she hid her looks behind a thick layer of makeup. She wore shorts, too high and tight, and a tube top that left her flat midriff exposed. Jenna had her work cut out for her. If she didn't keep a close eye on Brittany, the dozens of cowboys working the ranch would eat her alive.

Her brother, Brad, was around the same age as her trainees, but he'd filled out nicely, already what she'd consider a man in appearance. He even passed Mr. Wagner in height.

"Is that how you greet your host?" Ms. Scarlett scolded.

Brad's hand shot out to shake Mr. Wagner's. "Good to meet you, sir."

"Brittany?"

Before turning to face them, the girl rolled her eyes. She leaned in and offered a sorry excuse for a hug.

"Beautiful children. Just beautiful." Mr. Wagner beamed. He'd always loved being a father, dreamed of having more children before his rodeo accident so many years ago. Jenna knew he'd be in his element having friends and family around the ranch until the weekend wedding. Her heart swelled seeing her boss so content. Family and weddings were never meant to be part of her life, so she'd live vicariously through him.

Chapter Two

Trevor had just finished delivering a trailer of young cattle, then Jenna sent him back out to pick up supplies for the damn wedding. Enough food to feed an army had already arrived, but they still needed more of everything. By dinner hour, he was exhausted and just wanted to head to his trailer out back to crash.

He did his usual rounds to ensure the cattle were secure and horses were settled. Trevor took his job as foreman seriously. He may have had a few rough years as a teenage runaway, but since coming to the ranch and being mentored by Mr. Wagner, he'd made a complete turnaround of his life.

The first run of farmhands was already inside having dinner. He'd catch the second run because he wanted to hit the shower first. As he made his way through the open center of the barn, he used his Stetson to sweep away the loose dust covering his jeans.

"Hey, cowboy." The sweetly feminine voice took him by surprise. He looked up to find God's gift to men leaning against one of the empty stalls.

"And who would you be?" He replaced his hat onto his head after running a hand through his tousled hair. The woman raking her eyes up and down his body was young and ripe. His cock hardened.

"My mother dragged me here for a wedding. I don't want to be here…but maybe I've been too hasty." She sashayed closer until only a foot separated them. "I've always had a weakness for cowboys."

"What's your name, darlin'?"

She walked her fingers up his chest, playing her flirting game. He had no problem taking whatever she offered. Trevor wasn't married.

If a hot little number wanted a good time, he'd show her one. There hadn't been a single woman on the ranch since Grace had stayed for a month, and that had been nearly a year ago. With the heavy demands from the ranch, especially with seasonal workers in short supply, he rarely got a chance to head into town to look for action. He'd been walking around so pent up and snappy lately that even Jenna was becoming a distracting temptation.

"Brittany." Her green eyes looked up at him with feigned innocence. He knew this girl was anything but sugar and spice, but that didn't concern him.

"That's a pretty name, sweetheart." He tucked her hair behind her ear, leaning in to see how close he could get. "You look lost."

"You gonna show me around, cowboy?"

He moved in, pressing her against the boards separating the stalls. She gave him every signal he needed—she was his. He'd take her back to the trailer and fuck her proper. The evening had taken a sharp turn for the better.

"I'll show you something you've never seen before—"

"Hey! What on God's green earth is going on in here?" He turned to find Jenna standing in the center of the barn with her hands on her hips. Her scowl was enough to make him cringe. "Mansfield?"

"Just saying hello to one of our guests." He pulled away, wishing he could adjust the erection straining against his unforgiving blue jeans. "Shouldn't you be helping Pete or something?" Of all the times to show up.

"Actually, I'm in charge of all Mr. Wagner's guests, including your next victim here." She stormed over and wrapped a hand around Brittany's upper arm, tugging her close. Was she jealous that Trevor was about to get lucky with that fine piece of ass and she wasn't? Imagining Jenna and Brittany getting freaky together didn't help his uncomfortable position. He shifted, trying to alleviate the pressure in his pants.

"Victim? I didn't see her complaining, darlin'."

"Don't darlin' me, foreman. You should know better." She began her departure, hand still around the girl's arm. Jenna turned back with a heated glare. "You're on my list, Mansfield."

Great. There went his evening plans. Now he'd be painfully pent up until he had a chance to get to town, which wouldn't be any time soon. Jenna sure knew how to dampen a party. She probably wanted Brittany for herself. He'd never seen her with a girlfriend, and she rarely left the ranch. Now she was gunning for him on top of everything else.

* * * *

Only a few hours after Ms. Scarlett's arrival and the cowboys were already sniffing around her daughter. Jenna didn't know how she'd maintain order for another four days. There was no way in hell she'd let the hired hands get their paws on Brittany. She was too cute for her own good, and Jenna knew she was trouble from the moment she saw her. But Jenna had firsthand knowledge of how easily young girls could lose their way, and she wouldn't turn a blind eye while Brittany degraded herself for attention.

She attempted to tug her arm free of Jenna's grasp, so she released her. "I'm not a child. I can look out for myself."

"These aren't the type of men you're used to. They only know how to take."

Brittany exhaled her displeasure as they neared the house. "They ain't taking if I'm giving."

Jenna stopped short before reaching the kitchen doors. "Listen to me—you're not going to embarrass your momma or Mr. Wagner while you're here. This is supposed to be a time of celebration, and I won't have you ruin it."

"Who the hell are you anyway? You don't look much older than me."

They may be close in years, but Jenna was double her age from life experience.

"I'm not your enemy, but you'd be smart to take my advice. I've been living here for six years and know about everything that goes on around this ranch."

She chuckled, a satisfied smirk on her face. "Oh, I get it. You want him for yourself."

Jenna tensed, her defenses nipping at her. "Trevor? Don't get smart. I'm able to work with all these cowboys because I'm not into men. They know it, so they don't mess with me. You, on the other hand, you're like a flame to moths, or rather a piece of meat to the coyotes."

"A lesbian? Really? I'm surprised Mr. Wagner hired you. He's as old-fashioned as my mother. Did he bring in a priest to try and convert you?"

Jenna shook her head and smiled. "Come on, I know we'll be friends yet." She hooked an arm with the girl, and they entered the patio doors leading into the kitchen. The long rectangular wooden table was covered with plates of steaming food—grilled steak and chicken legs, fresh-made rolls, corn, mashed potatoes and gravy—and surrounded by cowboys. The near-deafening multitude of conversations stopped abruptly once she closed the doors behind them. All eyes focused on Brittany.

Heathens—every last one of them. "Should I tell Mr. Wagner you're looking at his young guest in an unholy way?" Jenna preferred having no women visit the ranch because the crew of cowboys really were like animals with no self-control. You'd think they'd never seen a woman in their lives. Having them gawk at Brittany brought back memories of Grace's stay at the Wagner ranch. Jenna wasn't so naïve. She knew what the men had done with Grace behind her back, including Trevor. Sex was the only thing on their minds, and they'd never change. They wouldn't get so lucky with Brittany. This time Jenna was wise to their tricks.

Brittany flirted with the men, teasing and taunting as Jenna pulled her through the kitchen as fast as she could. She ignored their whistles and indecent proposals for now. Ms. Scarlett and the other guests could be in earshot, so she didn't want to cuss the cowboys out, but she would. Mr. Wagner wanted the workers on their best behavior, and so far they had only made fools of themselves.

"I'm twenty-one. If I want to have a little fun, you shouldn't try to stop me," Brittany complained once they were safely in the hallway and out of sight.

"Have all the fun you want, but screwing around with the ranch hands is out of the question. Once you go back home, you're free to do as you will."

"I'll be in my room!" She twirled and stomped off down the long hallway in a snit. So much for friendship. Grace had been so much easier to get along with—shy, sweet, and desperate for reassurance. Brittany was a spoiled rich girl in need of an attitude adjustment, and probably a good spanking.

Jenna had already showed the guests their rooms earlier. All her duties for the night were done. It was time to disappear until morning. She avoided the kitchen even though she needed to give those cowboys a much-needed tongue-lashing. It was late, and exhaustion pulled at her. Since the wedding planning had begun, her responsibilities around the ranch had tripled, not to mention she still had to train her two greenhorns. They ate enough to feed an army and enjoyed dicking around the farm—but did nothing that resembled work. She'd shape them up or ship them out in a hurry because nobody got a free ride on the Wagner Ranch.

Slipping out the heavy front doors, she escaped into the balmy summer evening. The sun had set, but the sky remained a canvas of deep blues and purples. The drone of insects surrounded her, lulled her. She focused on the sound of her boots crunching the gravel along the well-worn path leading to the main barn. It was nice when things were this quiet. She inhaled deeply, filling her lungs with sweet country air.

Jenna was the only woman living on the Wagner ranch. Being open with her sexuality helped keep the men away, but her "don't fuck with me" attitude ensured they didn't hit on her. She wouldn't dare share a trailer with the ranch hands, or Conner's cottage at the rear of the property. Instead, she had her own little piece of heaven in the rear loft of the main barn. It was small, but cozy—her own little retreat. Mr. Wagner had offered her a room in the house because, like he said, he really did treat her like the daughter he never had. She respectfully refused, preferring her privacy. So he renovated her current apartment from extra hay storage to custom bachelorette.

"Nice evening." The male voice originated in the long shadows along the side of the barn.

"It's lovely, so don't ruin it, foreman." She knew Trevor would be pissed with her after stealing away his bedmate. Normally, she'd care less about his extracurricular activities, but she wouldn't risk tarnishing the wedding.

He stepped away from the wood plank wall and held up both arms in surrender. "No problem here." Then he smirked, his eyes holding secrets.

"What're you up to?"

"Brittany's cute, isn't she?"

"I suppose."

He studied her reaction for a moment. "How about we flip for her? Wagner doesn't have to know, and I know she won't say a word." He pulled a quarter from the small pocket in the front of his tight blue jeans.

"You're nuts." She hurried away from him, too tired for his games.

His heavy footfalls shattered the comforting silence. "Hey! Wait up!"

He blocked her path with an arm braced against the side of the barn, forcing her to deal with him. Trevor was difficult to ignore, standing nearly a foot taller than her. "I don't want to 'flip' for her. If she weren't Ms. Scarlett's daughter I'd let you have your fill, but she is, so stay away."

Trevor dropped his arm, not promising to stay away from the girl, but also not continuing to challenge her. "Guess I'll see you at sunrise then." He raked his eyes up and down her body. Surely he didn't notice that her nipples pebbled when his arm brushed against them. She only wore loose flannel, anything to stay off the radar.

Jenna took a cleansing breath as she walked away from him. Before climbing the ladder to her loft, she called back, "I suggest you take a cold shower to forget that girl, foreman, because we have a busy day tomorrow and I need you at your best."

* * * *

As the days passed, Jenna kept her promise and had Wagner's guests under constant supervision. Trevor had seen Ms. Scarlett's daughter again when she took a tour with her brother on horseback. If he just had her alone for half an hour, he'd take her hard and fast against the side of the barn. Nobody would be the wiser.

It was now only two days until the big wedding. Trevor began to feel the weight of his title heavy on his shoulders, which helped distract him from his libido. As foreman, Wagner expected him to keep control of the workers and maintain order in the thriving cattle business. He did his job well, but he was understaffed and overworked. Jenna still hadn't trained the greenhorns enough to be more a benefit than a liability. Having the branding and the wedding the same week was bad timing, but both needed to happen, so he manned up and pushed himself harder.

"Does that hurt the cow?"

Trevor turned, hot brand in hand. "It's like a tattoo. Only hurts for a second."

Ms. Scarlett's son looked to be similar to his age. He sat on the top rung of the fence wearing a polo shirt and khaki shorts. Trevor doubted he worked a man's day in his life. Their father had been as wealthy as Mr. Wagner before he died, and left all his money to Ms. Scarlett and their two children. Trevor really resented people, especially men, who had everything handed to them on a silver platter. Real men worked for everything they had, unlike Scott and Brad.

"Looks painful." Trevor ignored Brad and branded the calf's rump with the Wagner seal before swatting it on its way to join the others. He couldn't entertain one of the guests and expect to get another hundred branded before lunch. Where was Jenna? Wasn't she supposed to be playing hostess to all these guests?

Trevor tried to be civil. "Would you like to try?" In fact, he'd been on friendly terms with Scott since the whole Grace fiasco. Being bitter got him nowhere, so he made an effort more often than not these days. "It'd be something to tell your friends back home."

Brad smiled and hopped into the pen. He was about as tall as Trevor and not skinny like the greenhorns. If he were a cowboy, he'd make a good addition to their crew. "You know what I'd like to brand? That blonde cowgirl—what's her name again?"

Trevor frowned. "You talking about Jenna?"

"That's her. Fucking sweet. Is she single?"

For some reason Trevor's hackles rose. Jenna belonged to the Wagner ranch, and he didn't want to share. Nobody dared to talk about Jenna like a piece of meat, besides horsing around. It felt odd. It felt wrong. "Hasn't anyone told you that she's gay? Don't waste your time."

"A lesbian? No way. That's just an excuse used by women that've never had a real man."

The cocky bastard reminded him of himself, so he didn't appreciate the target of his attention being Jenna, even if she could take care of herself. Why did he care? He'd known her for six years. They worked side by side as a team on countless occasions. She was a hardworking, trustworthy worker. Not unlike Wagner—she was tough, but compassionate.

"If I were you, I'd stay away from Jenna. She's a tough nut to crack."

"Maybe I'm the one for the job."

He wanted to say more, to warn him of her expertise behind the barrel of a gun, but thought better. It would be fun to watch Jenna cut this clown down to size.

Chapter Three

The rest of the week flew by in a whirlwind of wedding preparations, guest arrivals, and the usual demanding work of the cattle business.

"Look at me!" shouted Brad as he balanced along the top rail of the fence. His tie was undone and shirt buttons partially open. The only light highlighting his fool behavior were the spotlights scattered around the property. Even the moon dared not make an appearance, hiding behind thick cloud cover.

"You're drunk, Brad. Get down before you get hurt."

Jenna was glad that after the wedding tomorrow, things would finally go back to normal around the ranch. This had to be the worst night yet, thanks to Scott's bachelor party. It seemed every cowboy for a ten-mile radius was at the Wagner Ranch, drunk and rowdy. Tonight she kept her nine millimeter in the waistband of her jeans. The rest of the partygoers had to turn in their weapons before the alcohol was released or she had no doubt shots would be ringing out in the dead of night, spooking the cattle and unsettling the horses. It was crazy to allow the men to get this carried away. She tried to watch them like a hawk, making sure they did no damage to the property and didn't offend the sober guests staying at the house.

"I knew you cared about me," he sang, looking up at the full moon with a vacant smile.

For the love of God. Where was Trevor? She expected that as foreman he'd keep track of the men, even if it was off working hours.

"You'll ruin your suit for the wedding." She tried to reason with him, but decided it was pointless. His logic was lost at the bottom of a bottle.

She carefully navigated her way through the dark landscape, weaving between the cattle in the pen. The women had some sort of tea party earlier in the evening, but she declined their offer to attend. She wasn't one for lace and teacups. Instead, she chose to try and maintain some order as case after case of liquor and beer turned up empty.

"There she is," said Steve, appearing from the pitch-black interior of the barn. His tie was undone, and his white shirt partially unbuttoned. She felt a presence behind her, and when she turned, the blast of alcohol on Tanner's breath struck her before she could focus on his glazed-over eyes.

"Looking for trouble?" asked Tanner. "Or a little fun?"

Jenna wasn't afraid, wasn't a victim. Not even a sliver of fear crept its way into her thoughts. "You boys are gonna regret this come morning," she warned low and steady. Her muscles were tense and ready.

"There're two of us and one of you, sweet thing." Steve was even younger than her, a boy in her opinion. Although they weren't as built as the regular cowboys, they could still overpower her in a heartbeat. Lucky for her, she was prepared for just such a situation.

"You can count. That's more skill than you've shown all week during training."

Steve scowled and reached for her shirt, tugging her toward him. "Little bitch." She reached for the waistband at her back, ready to shove the barrel of her gun under his chin and make him beg for forgiveness. But before her fingers could touch the cool metal handle, Steve was yanked away from her.

"I don't think she's interested, *cowboy*." Conner held Steve back with ease, his features set hard.

"Mind your business."

Conner twisted Steve around and slammed him against the side of the barn, rattling the wooden planks. Tanner took off running. "You wanna drink like a man, but you can't hold your liquor. You say you're a cowboy, but you can't even rope a calf." She could only see black-and-white images in the minimal lighting. Conner only wore a fitted, white tank top, the dark tattoos on his upper arms moving every time he flexed his muscles.

"I ain't got no beef with you, Conner." Steve struggled futilely. Conner was the biggest guy on the ranch. No one messed with him.

"You do now." Conner pulled him by the scruff of the shirt like a marionette and dragged him into the side shelter where they did the branding all day. Jenna followed. The embers in the cast iron fireplace still glowed red. He pushed Steve's back against the table, holding him down with a palm to his chest. Then he brought a hot poker around, aiming it directly in front of his line of sight.

"No!" Steve wailed and squirmed. He no longer carried his booze-induced bravado. "I wasn't gonna do nothin'. Honest!"

"Conner... Don't do it. He's not worth it." Jenna's heart raced. If anyone was capable of such madness, it was Conner. He was a cold, hard fighter. When he first pulled Steve off her, she wondered if her situation had gone from bad to worse before she realized Conner was trying to help her.

"Jenna, don't defend him. He's a no-good drunkard."

"He's a stupid kid. Let him go." She hoped to God he'd listen to her. Was he just as drunk as Steve? Would she be his next victim? Right now all that mattered was ensuring he didn't brand the greenhorn. If he did, Mr. Wagner could be looking at a lawsuit, Conner could lose his job, and a black shadow would hang over Grace's wedding—all things she wouldn't allow to happen on her watch.

He didn't move, didn't flinch for what felt like an eternity. Conner just held the red-hot poker in front of Steve's face, his mind a mile away. He taunted the kid until she was sure he'd piss himself. Then in a quick move, he stood straight and stepped aside. "Get out here!" His voice was its usual deep baritone. They shared eye contact after Steve scrambled away. Conner's face was shadowed, highlighting the sharp planes of his face and black goatee. Why the fuck was her pussy pulsing? Her traitorous body was confusing fear and sex, that's all.

"You drunk, too?"

He shook his head slowly, not taking his eyes off her. "Never touch the stuff."

"Well, thanks for that. Not that I needed saving or anything." She reached back and palmed her Colt, which eased her tension.

Then as mysteriously as he appeared, he returned to the night, probably heading back to his lonely cabin out back. She decided her best bet was to call it a day and hole up in her apartment. There wasn't much she could do at this hour, and Brad was a lost cause. She'd deal with the aftermath of the bachelor party in the light of morning. Although she'd never been in any real danger thanks to her hidden weapon, Steve's attack had her nerves on edge. Her body continuously sent mixed signals to her after the way Conner sized her up. She was used to cowboys looking at her with hunger in their eyes, regardless of whether or not she was interested in men—except Conner. He wasn't a saint. She'd heard about his sexual escapades from the other men, even stories of his hard-core BDSM fetish. Jenna wondered what he did with the women he brought to his cabin. When they faced off, his gaze wasn't sexual—it screamed possession, dominance, ownership. Her body heated remembering his dark eyes and hard-set features. But she'd never be owned.

She spared no time in returning to her loft and locking the door behind her. Once safely inside, she slumped against the door and exhaled until she felt dizzy. Her place was simplistic, functional, but it did have its charm. She loved the color blue, from the early morning sky to the evening twilight, and the walls surrounding her reflected that. Dropping her gun on the coffee table amongst her other weapons, she collapsed onto her oversized, worn couch. She stared up at the ceiling feeling a violent mixture of loneliness and confusion. Over the years she'd built up such impenetrable barriers and now wondered if the benefits outweighed the disadvantages. She'd never fall in love, never have children, and never have a life beyond the Wagner Ranch.

Soon even Grace would be out of her life, off to start a family with Scott at their own place away from the ranch. Over the years she'd seen countless cowboys leave to start families. Some stayed—like Trevor and Conner. Others never lasted a month, like her greenhorns. What did the future hold for her? Did everyone expect her to find a nice woman to settle down with in an unorthodox relationship? They had another thing coming if that's what they believed. She had no more desire for women than the ranch stud, Trevor, had for men. But that was her little secret, the one Mr. Wagner kept under lock and key as she requested. Wagner promised he could keep her safe without the lie, but she knew she couldn't handle unwanted advances. She'd had enough of that growing up.

A knock at her door forced her to sit up in rush. Nobody dared climb those stairs. They were hers. She grabbed her favorite rifle off the table, metal knocking against metal as she pulled it from the pile, and then rested it on her shoulder. If Steve had a sudden return of bravery after Conner disappeared, she'd give him a new reason to piss his pants. She swung open the door. Standing on the small three-foot-by-three-foot landing was Trevor. He pushed his way inside without invitation.

"Foreman, have you truly lost your mind this time?"

"Conner told me about that fucking kid giving you trouble." Why was he so angry? She wasn't exactly a damsel in distress. "Did he touch you?"

"What? No! What do you care anyway?"

"Just because you agreed to entertain Wagner's guests doesn't give them the right to hit on you. I warned that piece of shit to stay away, but obviously the boy doesn't have the common sense to listen. When I find him—"

"When you find him—nothing." She dropped her rifle back on the table and wandered away from him and took two mugs out of the cupboard in her kitchenette. The coffeemaker was set to warm, so she poured them each a mug, not concerned that her back was to Trevor. He may have had an unsavory past before coming to the ranch, but she trusted him. "I'm sure they're halfway to town by now. I'm more upset that I'll have to start training new ranch hands all over again."

"Ranch hands? Wasn't Ms. Scarlett's son the one bothering you tonight?"

She lowered her brow. "No, it was that limp dick, Steve. When I last saw Brad, he was pissed drunk. He's probably asleep in the barley fields."

"Oh." Trevor's body seemed to visibly loosen. "Well, them boys were good for nothing anyway. I was going to tell Wagner to cut them loose."

She passed him a mug. "You probably need this more than me," she said.

"Real men can hold their liquor." He smirked. She noticed that his eyes were as blue as her painted walls, and she forced herself to look away.

"Conner said he doesn't drink. Is that true?"

He sat on the arm of her sofa. "Guess he doesn't want to end up a drunk like his old man."

"But you do?"

"I'm not a drunk, Jenna. It was a fucking bachelor party. You should know better than to compare me to my father." He attempted to stand up, but she shoved him back down with a hand to the chest.

"Relax. Drink your coffee, foreman."

She reclined on the other end of the sofa, feeling oddly comfortable with Trevor in her private place. He was the first man besides Mr. Wagner to pay a visit. He'd been on the ranch longer than her, longer than anyone. When he was a runaway teen, Wagner took him in and gave him a chance. Mr. Wagner replaced the drunken, abusive father he had grown up with, providing a positive, loving role model. Now Trevor was at the top of his game as foreman. They were essentially two in the same, both rescues, making the Wagner Ranch their home.

"So what do you think about the wedding?" he asked after taking a sip of coffee.

She shrugged. "It's good for everyone. I'm happy for Grace."

"Yeah. I suppose."

Jenna shifted to sit higher on the sofa. "I knew about the two of you, you know. Did you love her?" Her heart clenched as she awaited his response.

"Love? No." He shook his head emphatically. "We were open about our feelings. I didn't love her, and she didn't love me." He paced the floor in front of her. "She loves Scott." He said it like a curse. She knew he'd always harbored jealousy over Scott since he was Wagner's real son, which was the status he coveted. But since Grace came back to the ranch, they seemed to get along.

"You don't think they're good together?"

"They're perfect. Too perfect. The whole happily ever after makes my stomach turn." He dumped the rest of his coffee into the sink and set his empty mug on the counter. "That'll never be me."

"Well, aren't you Prince Charming, Mansfield. I thought even you would appreciate a happy ending."

"My life hasn't been a fairy tale, darlin'. I gave up on dreams long ago."

She watched him pace and fidget. He was one of the most handsome men on the ranch—blond, blue-eyed with classic, rugged good looks. His worn blue jeans hung low on his slim hips. The rest of his body all lean muscle and tanned a golden hue. She'd seen him with his shirt off too many times to count, which didn't help her predicament. Her body heated being alone in the enclosed space with

Trevor. But she'd grown good at hiding her feelings and desires. Her entire life was an act, built to protect herself from predators. Although Trevor had turned out to be a good man, thanks to Wagner's example, he was a player through and through.

"What about me?" she whispered. "Should I give up on my dreams, too?"

He dropped down to one knee in front of her. She tensed and pulled back, giving herself some personal space. "You're the one person around here that deserves a happily ever after, Jenna." He reached out to touch her chin, but pulled back before he made contact. "There any girls out there you're interested in?"

Right. Her lesbian charade. It seemed foolish to continue with the lie, but it was necessary if she wanted to work at the Wagner Ranch. If the dozens of sex-starved cowboys knew she was straight, they'd hit on her constantly, treat her differently. She liked being one of the guys, invisible, safe.

"No." She didn't want to elaborate and dig her lie deeper. The moment felt honest and vulnerable, and she wouldn't ruin it with insincerity.

"What about that cute young thing, Brittany? I thought you liked her."

"Trevor, just because I don't want you messing with her doesn't mean I want her. She's a flighty young thing that's only looking for a good time. But you already knew that, didn't you?"

"You said my name." His smirk was too cute. His face so close to hers. What would it feel like if she ran her fingertips along his stubbled jawline? Would his full lips feel soft or firm to the touch?

She swallowed. "So?"

"You never say my given name. I like the way it sounds coming from you." Why was he looking at her like that? He thought she was a lesbian. Did he see past the lie?

Chapter Four

When Conner had told Trevor he pulled a young drunk off Jenna, he thought he'd lose his mind. That spoiled rich kid in the polo shirt kept flashing in his head, and he regretted being kind to him earlier. The kid had said he wanted a piece of Jenna and obviously kept his word. All Trevor saw was red.

He didn't care that Jenna had a no-visitors policy. He had to ensure she was safe and unharmed. She may be one tough cookie, but she was a tiny little thing. Lesbian or not, she was a woman and needed protecting. One thing he couldn't tolerate was a man abusing a woman. He'd hated it when he went to the city to fetch Grace away from her abusive ex-husband, and he hated it now that Jenna had been assaulted.

It must have been the combination of heightened emotion, alcohol, and the fact he hadn't been laid in weeks because a new desire ignited inside him. He'd always been attracted to Jenna. It would be impossible not to be. She had the most killer curves he'd ever seen on a woman. But that's as far as things went between them, a silent attraction. Now he felt a new pull. She looked so different off guard, in her own comfortable surroundings. Such a stark contrast to the kill-or-be-killed woman that lorded over the cowboys during the day.

When she said his name with her sexy Southern drawl, his cock hardened in an instant. He only realized upon hearing her say his name that she'd never said it before. It was always foreman, cowboy, or Mansfield. His name on her sweet pink lips was the sexiest thing he'd ever heard.

"Say it again."

"What?"

"Please. Say my name again." He was so close he could feel her warm breath. Although he should pull away before he did anything stupid, he moved in closer.

At first, he wasn't sure if she'd sock him or kiss him. Then she humored him. *"Trevor."*

"Fuck that sounds good."

"You're drunk. You should go." She pulled her legs around, stood, and brushed past him. The water began to run as she washed the two mugs, effectively ignoring him. What was he thinking? Even though he may feel a connection, she wasn't attracted to men. It wouldn't be any different than Conner expecting him to have an attraction for him. It wasn't going to happen.

"You'll be at the wedding then?" When she only nodded without turning around, he let himself out.

* * * *

Conner stirred in bed, his body complaining from a hard day's work. The sun peeked through the slats in the blinds, reminding him he had to get up for the wedding. If he didn't show up, Wagner would kill him. Besides, he was happy for Grace after what she went through with her ex. Although he'd given her little thought in the beginning, she had grown on him. Grace deserved a peaceful life with Scott, not the abusive life she led with her ex. No woman should ever be abused.

Jenna had delivered his suit the day before. She always had a handle on everything. If something happened on the Wagner Ranch, she knew about it. Well, he doubted she knew about the night he spent with Grace in his cabin. He'd rather Jenna show up at his door, but that was wishful thinking. Grace was too easy to dominate. Jenna would be a challenge. She was a feisty one that he'd love to break.

An hour later he was showered, shaved, and dressed. He felt stiff in the tailored suit and couldn't wait to get his casual clothes back on. Conner had lived life as a cowboy since before he could remember. Before he left home, he'd put in a man's day, keeping things running while his father was off trolling the bars, fall-down drunk. Although he expected to take over the family business when he came of age, when the time came, all he wanted to do was get as far away from the memories as possible. The daily beatings by leather belt, the violent rampages, and the verbal assaults—all focused on Conner and his mother. Thank God he had no younger siblings. He'd much rather work another man's farm, a good man's, like Wagner's.

Conner looked at his reflection in the mirror above his dresser. He'd trimmed his goatee and slicked his short, dark hair back. Why the fuck did he have to look like his bastard father? He scowled and grabbed his jacket off the end of the bed. All the ranch hands were given the day off to attend the wedding, but there were still a couple orders that Conner needed to speak with Mr. Wagner about. He wouldn't mind slipping away from the wedding early to handle the shipments. It would be an excuse to get away from the crowd.

He went around to the back door of the main house, hoping to find Wagner in his small office near the back entrance. The rear yard was in full chaos with hired caterers, florists, and wedding planners running around like headless chickens. He rolled his eyes and entered through the screen door unnoticed. Before he knocked on the partially closed office door, he heard voices. He recognized Jenna's voice, and her tone wasn't casual, so he stopped and listened.

"Whatever you choose, I'll support you, darlin'." Mr. Wagner's calm baritone was easily recognizable. It had soothed the beast within Conner too many times to count. "If you want to come clean, you won't have to worry about them cowboys. If they value their jobs, they'll treat my best lady with respect."

"Thank you. I think I'll hold off for now though. It's better if they think I like women. I've just been feeling conflicted lately."

"What in heaven's name has been bothering you?"

"I don't know. I guess the wedding got me thinking about the future. *My future.* I don't know if I'll ever be able to love a man. I don't think I can trust again."

"Sweet Jenna, you're young with your whole life ahead of you. Any man that you choose will be the luckiest cowboy in the country." There was a pause. Probably Wagner pulling her close as he often did. "Darlin', not every man is a monster. I hope I've shown you that over the years."

Jenna sniffled. "I love you," she said. "I don't know what I'd do without you."

"Dry those tears, darlin'. You look prettier than a summer rose." He heard a chair shift on the hardwood, so backed away from the door. "One day I'll be throwing a wedding for you. Mark my words."

Footsteps grew closer, so he rushed to the screen door and pretended to enter as Jenna left the office. She glanced in his direction briefly, her blue eyes watery and vulnerable. Before he could rake his gaze down her body, she bolted in the other direction without a word. *Never show your weakness.* Jenna was more like him than he cared to admit.

She was pretty—fucking hot was more like it. She wore a navy blue satin gown that highlighted her eyes. Her pale blonde hair was loose down her back and shoulders, reaching the curve of her ass. He'd never seen her hair down. It was always functional, in a ponytail or braid. Half the time he truly did see her as one of the guys. Not anymore. He thought about what Mr. Wagner had just said, which pulled a rare smile to his lips.

Rather than talk with his boss as originally planned, he followed Jenna down the hallway to the front of the house. She escaped into the kitchen, now teeming with life. Pete, round and jovial, and a small crew of chefs were preparing food for the evening meal. Pots were boiling over, steam rising to the roof where drying herbs and pots hung from the rafters. It was noisier than a cattle roundup. He stood taller than everyone and tried to spy Jenna over the crowd. The patio doors off the kitchen opened and closed. He only caught a brief glimpse of blue satin before she disappeared. Shit, she was gone. He wouldn't know what to say to her if he caught her anyway. Just seeing the feisty cowgirl in a vulnerable state brought out his dominant side and whet his sexual appetite.

Conner could envision her tied naked to his bed. Although he'd never fantasized about her much in the past, that all changed now that he knew her secret. Jenna was no lesbian, only hiding behind the lie to keep the cowboys from drooling all over her. Smart move, but there was more to it than that. Mr. Wagner said something about a man— probably a drunken asshole like his father.

* * * *

Trevor just pulled up in his pickup truck when he saw Jenna run from the kitchen doors toward the barn. Her blonde hair flowed loose behind her in a soft wave, highlighted by the sun. He had to blink a few times before he believed it was really her. The long, tight dress barely contained her full breasts. He parked the truck, slamming the door behind him as he went in pursuit. He wasn't sure why he kept trying to start something with a woman that would never want anything to do with him.

"Jenna!" he called out after she entered the barn.

She was nearly to the wooden ladder that led to her loft when she turned around. "What is it, foreman? Shouldn't you be dressed proper by now?"

"I needed to see what color you were wearing. You're the maid of honor, and I'm the best man—we should match."

She scowled and crossed her arms over her chest, plumping her breasts further. He couldn't look away even though he knew she'd hide him for staring at her cleavage. "I don't think you'd look good in blue satin."

"I just need my tie or shirt to match, that's all." Trevor licked his lips, his body lighting up at the sight of the feisty blonde.

She turned, took a few steps, and started to climb the ladder. "Just because we're both in the wedding party, doesn't mean anything. You won't be getting lucky—not even close. Hell would have to freeze over first." A couple more steps up. "Go get dressed and stop looking at my ass."

He ignored the last part of her request and watched her until she disappeared into her apartment, giving him the middle finger before she slammed the door shut.

"She's wicked." Conner's voice came from the entrance of the barn. He cleaned up well, all suited up and ready to go. Trevor better follow Jenna's advice and get washed up himself.

"You're telling me. A wolf in sheep's clothing, if ever I saw one."

"Actually, you're more right than you realize," Conner said as he stroked his neatly trimmed goatee. "I shouldn't say anything, but—"

"What?"

Conner motioned for him to follow with a slight wave of his hand. Once out of the barn and back at Trevor's pickup truck, Conner leaned in close and whispered, "She's not gay."

Trevor could only frown, not sure what game he was playing. "What are you talking about?"

"Jenna's not a lesbian. It's all a ruse. I overheard her talking with Wagner this morning. They're both in on it. She pretends to hate men. That way they don't bother her at work. Makes sense, right?"

He stood in quiet contemplation. The past six years played back through his head like an old movie. He tried to remember everything they'd been through together. His pulse quickened, and his muscles tensed. All these years he'd held nothing back. She probably thought he was a womanizer, maybe he had been. She knew all about his women, his sexual forays, his nasty habits. Knowing that she was straight changed everything in a single second. Their intimacy the other night wasn't one-sided like he believed. The lust and desire dancing in her eyes wasn't his imagination. *Un-fucking-believable!* The hottest chick he'd ever encountered was available, ready to be wooed—by him.

Trevor had to admit that his first thought was how quickly he could convince her to get naked and on her back. Not many women refused him. He just hadn't tried very hard where Jenna was concerned thanks to her brilliant little white lie. But then again, this was Jenna he was talking about, not some random tail. Why did Conner have to spring this on him now? His mind would be elsewhere the whole wedding.

"Who else knows?"

"Just you and me. I think it's best to keep it that way. Wagner would have our balls if he found out we spread word around the ranch." Conner tilted his head from side to side, attempting to loosen his collar. The man looked ready to rip the suit right off his body.

"Yeah." His mind wouldn't stop reeling. "If it's true, I call dibs."

"Fuck you. You can have her when I'm through."

"What makes you think she'll want you, Conner? She knows all about the real you."

"We'll see." He took in a deep breath and ran a hand through his dark hair. "It's the loud, mouthy ones that have a secret submissive side."

Trevor laughed, slapping the closed bed of the truck. "You're joking, right? If Jenna agrees to play some kinky game with you, I'll hand over next week's paycheck."

"A woman like that needs a real man, not a rodeo clown." He walked off toward the house after his cheap shot. He turned back, continuing to put distance between them. "If you think she'll fuck you and three of your boys like Grace did, you're the one who's full of shit."

Trevor wanted to argue, wanted to make a wager, but his mind was still processing the news. He couldn't tell Jenna he knew the truth, or she'd deny it and it would create an uncomfortable tension between them. They worked side by side most days, so he didn't want to put his job at risk. The Wagner Ranch was not only his place of employment, but also his home—his heart. Before he arrived at the front gates, his life had been a forfeit. He wouldn't risk his new existence, not even for a decadent treat like Jenna.

Chapter Five

The crowd had thinned after the reception. Jenna assisted Grace to her room to help her prepare for her honeymoon, holding up the layers of silk and taffeta in her arms.

"You excited?" Jenna unzipped the back of her heavy white gown.

"It's like a dream," she said. "I feel like I'm living the fairy tale." Grace covered her bare breasts once the material fell heavily around her feet. Jenna had to continually remind herself that everyone thought she was gay. She usually played the part, even with Grace—an extra-long look, or intimate touch here and there. Today, she couldn't even muster up the energy to fulfill her role. She felt bogged down, soul deep, searching for answers she'd never find. It was tough watching people you loved move on to better things while you stayed in the same place in time, never going forward because of a past you couldn't let go.

"You deserve it after what you went through with that asshole." Grace's ex, Ken, may be dead and buried, but he didn't deserve sympathy. Jenna couldn't stand men that felt they could control a woman, ruin a life to enhance their own. She'd been a victim herself and never stood by idly to watch a fellow female abused.

"I guess everything happens for a reason. I wouldn't have met Scott if it weren't for the wife swap, and there wouldn't be a wife swap if Ken were a good man." Grace sighed as she slipped on a cream-colored, simple dress. "Everything's connected if you think about it."

Jenna wondered what on earth could be positive about what she had to experience as a young woman at the hands of her own blood.

She finished helping out the woman she considered her closest friend. Grace was a fragile thing, and Jenna was glad she ended up with a stable man like Scott, so much like his father. He wasn't Jenna's type though. Like Trevor continually preached to the guys— Scott was too soft. Jenna would require a real man, a cowboy not afraid to get his hands dirty.

After helping her sort through her travelling bags, she left Grace in the attention of numerous guests that were getting ready to depart and slid out the side door into the night.

Grace and Scott were now a married couple and would soon be off to the airport by limousine to catch a plane for their honeymoon. Jenna wasn't a sentimental woman, but the ceremony had tugged at her heartstrings. She'd seen Grace before Scott came into her life, so lost and confused. Then she witnessed the transformation as they fell in love with each other. She tried to imagine herself in a white gown, standing at the altar with a man that looked at her with love burning in his eyes.

She shook her head, angry for her wayward thoughts. There wouldn't be a white dress for her because she wasn't pure—she'd been defiled in the worst way imaginable. What kind of man would want a woman who had been raped? It was disgusting, vile, and deviant. If she couldn't face the past, how could she ever open up to a lover? Better to live in denial and play her starring role that would keep her safe from men. She hugged herself as she watched the guests depart, car after car starting up and heading down the long, dark road leaving the property. There was a chill in the night air, goose bumps creeping up her bare arms. Her nipples pebbled from the cold, reminding her of her shame. If she weren't so damn buxom, the bastard may have been able to resist her. Like her mother had said, she was a she-devil, a tease, a home-wrecker. Tears pricked at the backs of her eyes. She hated that her parents could still affect her even now. Why couldn't she move on?

She didn't want to dwell on the past. Wagner offered her a chance at a new life, and she gladly accepted. But forgetting the pain that cut her soul deep wasn't as easy as she had hoped. If she could physically remove the memories, she'd carve them out of her body with a rusty blade.

"Cold night to be out here without a sweater." She spun around, still hugging herself. Trevor leaned against one of the oak trees lining the long driveway. He wore his black suit, the one that had captured her attention all evening. The man looked edible in formal wear. He'd lost the jacket and tie somewhere along the way, now in just his pants and a partially opened shirt that matched her dress. Her connection to him from the other night came back after a single glance at his face. Trevor emitted a calm energy. He was a laid-back cowboy, not easy to rile.

"I was just—"

"Thinking?"

"I guess. The wedding's over now. Life will go back to normal."

He slowly exhaled, rubbing behind his neck. It had been a long day, and she felt the strain herself. "I'll be glad. It's been crazy the past week."

Back to normal. She couldn't help but see the future as bleak, loveless, pointless. After a good night's sleep, she'd strengthen her emotional barriers and forget about the vulnerability threatening to undo her tonight. She'd focus on work and making Wagner proud.

She straightened her back and concentrated on maintaining her composure. "I'll have to ask around about getting some new ranch hands. In the meantime I'll help out with the branding."

"Good. We'll get a hell of a lot more done without those clowns."

"You can go back to parking the trucks at the front now." She began to walk away from him, too tempted to let it all go. "I'll be busy as hell tomorrow helping Pete with the cleanup, but after that I'll help out with the cattle."

"You're the best, darlin'."

She shook her head in annoyance, finding it difficult to be hostile when she was drained of emotion. "Don't darlin' me, cowboy."

As she put distance between them, she heard his quick footfalls behind her. She turned sharply. Trevor put up his hands and stopped dead. "Those yellowbellies may still be lurking around. I should escort you back to your room."

"Escort me?" She chuckled. "Since when did I need your help, Mansfield? Save the dramatics for your buckle bunnies."

Jenna began walking again, Trevor at her side like a pain in the ass. "You're a woman."

"And—"

"You need a man to take care of you."

She ground her molars together. There was a fine line between being gallant and being an asshole, and Trevor just crossed it. Even being nearly a foot shorter, she pushed him in the chest with force. "Do I look like I need a man? Do I look like a helpless woman?" The satin of her gown caught her eye as the spotlights shimmered off the surface. "Okay, I look like one tonight, but once this dress comes off, you'll remember who I really am."

"Who might that be?"

"A cold, hard bitch that you'd be wise not to mess with. I don't need, nor do I want, a man, and you know it." He just stood staring down at her. She was making a fool of herself, so took a cleansing breath and slowed her breathing. "Forget it. I'll see you in the morning, bright and early."

Once she reached the barn, Trevor was still rooted in place where she'd left him. They exchanged a long glance before she escaped into the dark interior of the barn.

* * * *

Trevor had to bite his tongue. He wanted to shout out that he knew who she really was. He wanted to shut her up with a mind-numbing kiss, feel her soft body pressed against his. Her bravado was partially an act. He knew that now. It took all his resolve to keep his newfound knowledge locked within. How long could he keep this secret? Mr. Wagner knew. Conner knew. Would Conner make his move before him? Did the guy really believe he could dominate that wild filly?

He'd seen a softer side to her tonight—the other night, too. Should he confront her with what he knew? Would she even want him? Maybe the kindest thing he could do was forget about her and carry on with his job at the ranch. He knew damned well he wasn't ready to settle down. Jenna didn't deserve to be treated as disposable. Besides, she'd have his balls if he broke her heart. He smiled. As much as he should stay away, his feet led him to the barn and the ladder leading to her apartment. He truly was a fool.

Trevor knocked at the door, ready for the tongue-lashing of a lifetime. He held his breath when the door opened, cutting the darkness on the small landing. She'd been crying. Only a few minutes alone and she'd been crying, her eyes red-rimmed and moist. What had he said wrong?

"You okay, Jenna?"

"Of course I'm okay," she snapped. "What are you doing here? It's late."

"You've been crying."

She shook her head, averting her gaze to the floor. The lighting coming from within was soft, probably from a lone table lamp. "I'm just overly tired."

Without asking permission, he pressed into her apartment, forcing her backwards, and closed the door with his boot. She sniffled and continued to move away from him until her back hit the wall. He filled her personal space, prepared for a fight because he'd seen this before. She was more like a man than she realized, bottling up her feelings until ready to explode. He'd let her use him to vent her emotion, even if he turned black and blue. The tension was thick, and he could feel her nerves like tight bowstrings. Any minute she'd snap, and that's exactly what she needed to do.

"Trevor..."

"There's my name again. It sounds sweet on your lips, darlin'."

She whispered, her words holding little conviction. "I told you never to darlin' me."

"You looked beautiful tonight. The prettiest girl in the bunch." He dared to tilt her chin up. Her blue eyes were deep pools to get lost in. Her hostility fizzled away when he expected it to fire hot.

"I'm not a girl," she insisted. "I'm like you, like any other ranch hand."

"Wrong." He pressed in closer until only inches separated them. She'd changed clothes fast, already out of the blue satin and wearing flannel pajama bottoms and a loose T-shirt. Her long, blonde hair was yet to be tied back, flowing softly over her shoulders. "You're very much a woman, Jenna." He was careful, speaking each word slowly and gently. She needed to understand the truth behind his words. Whether she played a man's role or not, she was still a woman, and a stunning one at that.

Something would happen soon. The Jenna he knew well would have socked him in the gut by now and never have let him get so close to her. Her rifles were only a dash away, and she knew how to use them. She allowed herself to be cornered.

Her chest rose and fell in deep, rapid waves. She swallowed hard, forced to look him in the eye when he held her attention. "What do you want from me?"

"Everything."

She shook her head in rapid denial. "Damn it, Trevor! You know me. You can't come in here and expect me to lie down and spread my legs just because you have a hard-on."

"But you will."

"Fuck you, foreman." She shoved him, but his body was like a wall to a slight thing like her. "I like women, get it? Men repulse me, and it's no wonder why."

He leaned down and kissed her on the lips, just enough to shut her up, then backed off. With her jaw slack, she just stood staring at him. When she did nothing to push him away, he returned to her lips, slow enough that she could refuse him if she chose to. He kissed her softly, tasting her lips and enjoying the softness.

"Still hate me?" he said against her lips.

"More." Her lips moved against his now, kissing back with caution. When her sweet little tongue licked along the seam of his lips, he was forced to pull back and take a breath. His cock burned in his pants, never so eager to fuck a woman before.

"You're holding back," he said.

"So are you, if all your stories are true."

"Oh, they're true." He brushed her hair from her shoulder, smoothing it down her back. She flinched and tensed, uncomfortable with the intimate contact. God, how long had she gone without a man's touch? "What about you? That was a mighty fine kiss from a woman that claims to have sworn off men."

"It's just a kiss."

He ran his finger along the neckline of her shirt, tempted to go for the gold and manhandle her perfect, full breasts. *Breathe, Trevor.* He trailed his fingertips down the length of her arms until he reached her hands. She attempted to tug her hands free of his, but he held fast. "I've been fantasizing about this for years, you know."

"Figures. No matter how hard I try, you still see me as a piece of ass."

"I'm a man, Jenna. I'd be a fool not to appreciate you for what you are." He lowered his head, desperate to nuzzle her neck, to become lost in her scent. "You do wicked things to my body."

She tilted her head to the side, allowing him to suck her pulse point and nip at her ear. A sigh trembled from her lips, but she was quick to stifle it. "Coming from you, that's not a compliment. A change in wind can turn you on, cowboy."

"Nothing short of a beautiful woman can do this to me." He pressed her hand to his erection, now harder than the wall he pressed her against.

"Shit, that's hard." They both laughed. They'd been working together too long to play games with each other. She knew him inside and out, knew about his sexual forays, and didn't put up with his bullshit. The fact that they shared this intimacy already boggled his mind. How could he ever use her and walk away? This was Jenna— the tough chick that managed to keep dozens of cowboys in line, the girl Wagner considered a daughter and Trevor's secret wet dream for the past six years.

Chapter Six

Jenna was *lost, lost, lost*. What had she done? Trevor, the ranch's biggest playboy, was in her apartment, kissing her, touching her. Her entire lesbian charade since arriving on the Wagner ranch was to keep sharks like him away from her. Cowboys were too hard-core and would only hurt her when she needed to heal. If she ever healed at all.

It would be too easy to toss him out with a hard kick to the ass, so why hadn't she? The wedding certainly pulled down her carefully guarded barriers, but it was more than that. She harbored a secret crush for the foreman. He was sexier than sin and a hard worker. Jenna worked with the men and could appreciate a real man, a skilled cowboy that wasn't afraid of hard work or getting hurt. The image of some soft-skinned rich boy repulsed her. Trevor was everything she dreamt a man should be and more. But men took without giving back. How many stories did she have to hear before she realized he'd only use her like all the others?

When the laughter died away and she pulled her hand back, his eyes darkened, and a new intensity pulled her in like a calf being roped. "Fuck, Jenna, I need you. Don't stop touching me."

His cock was hard and thick, even through his suit pants. Her curiosity soared, but her protective instincts told her to back off. "I can't."

"Let me touch you then." The image of Trevor's rough hands all over her bare skin made her nipples tighten into bundles of nerves. Her pussy clenched, and she gasped from the need that suddenly took over. She didn't stop him when he snagged the edge of her T-shirt or when he pulled it off over her head.

The chill in the room became noticeable once she stood topless, in just the tight sports bra she used to rein in her unruly breasts. "Fuck. Me. I knew you'd look good, but not this fucking good." He groaned and palmed her breasts through the white cotton material. Her pussy pulsed as he kneaded her sensitive flesh.

"They're too big." It was a fact. For being barely five feet with a petite figure, her DDs were out of place and a constant torment.

"You're perfect. So soft and sweet and perfect." He bent down, peeled the cup over one breast down, covering her areola with his hot, wet mouth. Jenna cried out, not ready for such an explosion of sensation. He buried his face in her soft mound while teasing her nipple.

"Trevor!"

"Mmm, say my name, baby." She did, over and over, as he assaulted her body with the skill of an expert lover. With both bra cups now peeled down, her breasts were thrust up and inward, creating a mountain of cleavage that Trevor appeared to enjoy partaking in. His tongue was cruel and magical. Her entire body lit up with a new heat, a wondrous warmth filled her veins and stole her inhibitions.

As he continued to suckle her, he tugged down her pants, leaving her completely naked. She felt so exposed, but it was titillating. Then she thought better. "Mansfield, I hope you plan to get naked yourself."

He stood and smirked. "Yes, ma'am." Trevor undid his shirt buttons one at a time, torturously slow, while maintaining eye contact with her. She could feel a liquid heat seep from her body and trickle down her inner thigh. Her entire body felt like a coiled spring.

Once unbuttoned, she helped him, pushing the blue material off his very broad shoulders. She'd noticed his muscled frame from all the times he worked shirtless. But she'd never been able to acknowledge her feelings or get an up-close-and-personal inspection. His pecs were firm and defined, a thick cord of muscle running from his neck along his shoulders. He tensed when she ran her palms down his chest to his washboard stomach. Unlike her fair skin, he was hard and golden from working under the sun. So this was how a man was supposed to feel. Jenna savored his firm, muscled flesh under her inspection.

His shirt fell to the ground, and she wrapped her hands around his belt. Did she have the nerve to strip him completely? "Go on, darlin'. I can't wait another second."

She pulled the belt free of his buckle and unzipped his pants. The heavy weight of the designer slacks slipped down his narrow hips, leaving him in just black boxer briefs. Would she go through with this? Could she?

Before she could make a move, he reached behind her, cupping her ass and lifting her against him with ease. He carried her to her twin-sized bed, neatly made with a patchwork quilt, and fell over her. His heat, his weight, his flesh against hers made her world spiral out of control. She no longer cared about Trevor's reputation or hers after tonight. The only thing that mattered was living in this blissful state of complete sexual abandon. Her head cleared of worries, of pain, like a drug had been infused into her blood from his first kiss.

They kissed now, deeply, passionately. He tasted so alive, all male, and delicious. Would she ever have her fill? Trevor easily removed his boxers without pulling away, and then his thigh parted her legs further. "I can't wait to get inside you," he groaned, positioning his cock at her entrance. Already drowning in an overflow of moisture, he coated himself in her juices, sliding back and forth between her folds. The friction drove her mad, made her desperate to be filled to the brink with his thick cock. Her clit pulsed even without direct contact.

He pressed in an inch, stretching her. "Fuck you're tight." She'd only been penetrated once before, and she didn't want to think about that now. Sex with Trevor would erase those memories, replace them with something that wasn't violently forced upon her.

She cringed and tightened around his length as he thrust slowly forward. He leaned back to look her in the eyes as he filled her. "I want you to enjoy yourself."

Jenna didn't want pity. She wasn't afraid of sex—sex couldn't control her. "Then make me feel good." She loosened her grip on his dick, willing her muscles to relax and melt into the mattress. As soon as she calmed herself mentally, Trevor worked her body, thrusting in and out of her pussy in long, smooth strokes. The sensations pricked at her nerves, sending a tingling goodness to all her extremities. She wrapped her arms around his warm shoulders and held on, savoring the intimacy, savoring the way sex should be. His body was warm, skin to skin against her own. She felt surrounded, protected, but thought better—sex was a bad thing.

Despite her attempted control, panic crept into her blood. She wanted this, enjoyed this, but couldn't control the way her mind reacted.

"Stop!" she squealed, out of breath.

"Did I hurt you, darlin'?"

She exhaled and dropped her head back, staring at the ceiling. No way could she tell Trevor she was scared. Weakness wasn't tolerated at the Wagner Ranch and certainly not by her. She shook her head.

"I know just the thing." He winked, kissed her lips once, and slipped out of her body. She felt empty once his cock was removed, sending her into a violent muddle of emotions. Trevor crawled back down her body and peppered kisses along her inner thigh. The area was so sensitive to his ministrations that she gasped and unconsciously thrust her pelvis up. "That's a girl. I can't wait to taste you sweet little cunt."

Trevor moved closer and closer to her throbbing clit. When he latched his mouth over her pussy, she called out and tangled her hands in his mop of dirty-blond hair. A new pressure began to rise, spreading heat up from the tips of her toes. She concentrated on the new pleasure coursing its way through her body towards her center.

Trevor's tongue was no less skilled than any other part of him. He nipped and suckled her clit, lapped at her folds, and fucked her with his tongue. She lost all control, all fear, and braced herself for something monumental. Gripping the sheets, it came to a peak. She gasped in short breaths before her cunt exploded in a violent wave of extreme pleasure. Liquid flowed from her pussy, and it pulsed hard and demanding, but there was nothing there to fill it. God, she needed Trevor now.

"Hurry up and fuck me, cowboy!"

He complied, rising before falling over her and thrusting deep into her slick pussy. She exhaled in relief as he claimed her, her body still contracting around him as he fucked her good and hard. Once the tremors eased, she felt a new heat building, and she eagerly wanted to feel that burst of pleasure again. Jenna wrapped her legs around his hips, spurring him on. His body broke out in the fine sheen of sweat which she leaned up to lick off his shoulders before sucking the firm flesh on his neck. She had the urge to mark him as hers as a warning for any riffraff to stay away. *Hers.* Jenna suckled hard enough to leave a healthy mark on his neck and dropped back down to enjoy his sinful assault.

"Hurry up, sweet thing. I can't hold on forever." His breathing hitched, his thrusts coming harder, faster. "Come for me, Jenna."

Hearing her name on his lips was all she needed to reach her second peak. Her cunt milked his cock, and it felt immeasurably more satisfying to orgasm around his thick girth. Trevor groaned and sucked air in through his teeth as he pumped his seed into her body until he finally collapsed to his side.

She stayed on her back, enjoying the after-sex bliss as her breathing regulated. Trevor leaned to his side and ran his fingers along the valley of her breasts. "It was better than I imagined."

Now that it was all said and done, the cloud of lust that had blinded her, lifted. She felt an uncomfortable vulnerability slipping in, and she hated it. Was she just one of Trevor's many fucks, now to be forgotten? He had no idea how monumental the sex act was for her. It was her first consensual experience, and for the first time she could see a future with a man. But she refused to be weak and beg for his love. She'd die single first.

* * * *

Trevor couldn't stop looking at her, touching her. She was like a new toy that he couldn't get enough of. But for once he wasn't just interested in her body, but every detail. Trevor wanted to know her story, what made her into the woman she was today. "So where'd you learn to shoot?" asked Trevor. They had pulled the blankets around them, and he savored the feel of Jenna in his arms. If only he'd known her secret sooner, he could have pursued her years ago. He'd have to thank Conner for spilling the news about her sexuality.

She hesitated, opening her mouth and stopping a few times. "Foster home."

"You? Why didn't you tell me before?" Trevor had been to foster homes. His youth was one disappointment after another until Mr. Wagner finally took him in and offered him a job. He'd been on the ranch since his teens. There were a lot of assholes in the world, but rather than letting that hate and pain control him, he used it as a catalyst for better things. He tried to stay positive, not by forgetting where he came from, but being thankful for where he was.

"Since when do I share my personal life with the staff?"

"I thought I was more than just a coworker." He ran his fingers up and down her back. Her skin was so fair and soft. The more time he spent with her, the more he saw her as a woman, feminine. Trevor wondered how their relationship would be affected after what they just shared. Would it be awkward working side by side?

"I'm very private about my life. It has nothing to do with you."

"Was it bad? The foster home?"

She shook her head. "No." After a deep breath, she continued, "The foster home was okay. The husband was a hunter. He'd always wanted a son, his wife a daughter. When they took me in, he treated me like a boy, put me to work, which was fine with me. He taught me how to hunt, how to use all types of firearms. I'm thankful for the years I was there."

"Why'd you leave?"

"Once I turned eighteen, the state said I was on my own, so I left and came here."

He tilted her face to look at him. "Looks like we both followed the same path to get here. Mr. Wagner must be a godsend."

Her smile was gentle and sweet as if reflecting on the man that changed both of their lives.

Trevor felt a sense of peace. He unlocked a vault into the softer side of Jenna, one he hadn't been sure she possessed. Without her harsh façade, she was stunning. Light blue eyes and the silkiest blonde hair he'd ever seen on a woman. Her nose was small and slightly turned up like a pixie—adorable. He kissed the tip of it, which earned him a frown. This woman was more starved for affection than Grace had been. He'd have to work extra hard to show he that she deserved good things in her life.

Chapter Seven

Large billows of dust obscured the distant landscape. The earth trembled as the next batch of cattle was herded into the holding pen for branding. Trevor stood on the bottom rung of the fence and directed the animals to the far end. Conner, Bryce, and three other cowboys raced around on horseback, keeping the animals from returning to the fields. Loud calls and whistles filled his ears. Once the far gate was closed, he hopped down, ready to start his day.

He was surprised to find Jenna already in the barn, pressing the rump of an agitated calf against the stall wall while administering the Wagner Ranch brand. She was a skilled cowgirl and never asked for help, even when she needed it. Her beautiful hair was once again in a functional ponytail, and her gorgeous curves were camouflaged by thick flannel and blue jeans.

"Darlin', I didn't know you were going to be helping out today." He swatted the calf away and moved closer to her, hoping for a morning kiss.

"Since when is it okay to call me *darlin'*, foreman?" Her expression held no humor. She was back to tough-as-nails Jenna, and he almost forgot about the sweet creature he had spent half the night with.

He scowled, unsure of her intentions. "You didn't mind last night."

"If you think you're gonna run around and blacken my name, it'll be the worst mistake you ever made in your life."

"Why would I do that?"

She scoffed. "I've heard your sex stories too many times to count, and I don't want to be one of them. If you think of me as a notch in your belt, I'll make sure you won't make another."

He chuckled. "A threat? Problem is I'd welcome your soft little hands on my dick. Even if it hurt."

She backed away from him, swallowed hard, but said nothing. The feisty little filly made his cock ramrod hard.

"You think I'm playing?"

"Jenna, like you said, you know me. I ain't afraid of much. You can't scare me away easily." He touched his neck, remembering her hickey. "I liked your little gift. If you were so concerned about hiding our relationship, you should have thought twice before planting this one on me."

She steamed and stomped. "So help me, foreman…" Her little fists balled at her sides. "It was all a mistake. One I won't make again."

The woman didn't know who she was dealing with. He was a cowboy, used to working a man's day. He got what he wanted, when he wanted it, and every minute he wanted Jenna more.

Trevor leaned in once she was trapped against the wooden stall boards. "Want me to suck those beautiful tits again? I'll do it right now if you ask nicely." Damn, the woman smelled sweet.

He should have expected the blow. Her balled fist planted deep in his gut, stealing his breath. She reared out of the stall and grabbed the red-hot brand from the hearth. Her smile was evil and sexier than hell itself. She walked in measured steps toward him, her blue eyes narrowed.

"If you liked my mark so much, how'd you like another? Cowboys don't feel pain, right?" She was just crazy enough to brand him. Lucifer's daughter had nothing on Jenna. He held up his arms and retreated.

"You piss her off already?" asked Conner as he strode into the barn with his horse by his side. "Go on, Jenna…I'm sure he deserves it."

She dropped the brand in a bucket of water with a sizzle and a release of steam. One more cold stare in his direction and she left the barn, shoulder-butting Conner on her way out even though he was twice her size. What the hell was that about? Did she regret what they shared? He knew he didn't. In fact, he couldn't stop envisioning their next encounter.

"What's up her ass?"

Trevor shook his head. "Nothin'."

"You didn't tell her we knew the truth, did you?"

He wet his lips, not one to lie. If he could, he'd shout from the roof for everyone to hear that he'd gotten a taste of Jenna. Nobody would even believe him it was so farfetched. But, like she said, she wasn't one of his buckle bunnies just curious about fucking a cowboy. She was much more—what she gave him was rare, special, not something he planned to handle carelessly. He figured they could still be friends, or friends with benefits. Trevor still got along great with Grace even though she was with Scott. Sex didn't have to change everything, but Jenna seemed hell-bent on hating him now. It's not like he used her. She was more than willing. He could still remember the sounds she made as he brought her to orgasm again and again.

"Trevor!"

"Huh?" He couldn't even think straight. Why couldn't he get Jenna off his mind? He'd get himself killed if he didn't get focused soon. His job was dangerous, and he needed a level head and fast reflexes. "You say somethin'?"

"You did, didn't you? You told her!" Conner dragged a hand through his dark hair and exhaled in irritation. "I had a plan, and you fucking blew it for me."

"I didn't say anything, but if your plan was to get her to play your twisted games, think again. She's not the type of woman to submit. Trust me."

He grunted, exuding confidence. "Maybe not to you, but I can handle her and was looking forward to the challenge." Conner walked his horse to a stall and settled it in.

* * * *

Jenna's heart pounded so hard behind her ribs she swore she'd be able to hear it if it weren't for the deafening noise of the cattle clamoring for space in the pen and the rowdy cowboys around her. In the light of day she was certain Trevor would try and play off what happened between them. He rarely spent more than a week with one woman. She earned her tough reputation after years of putting roughneck cowboys in their place, and she wasn't about to lose it. Jenna refused to be the loose woman spoken about around the bonfires. If she could turn back time and never have opened the door for Trevor, she would, even if it was one of the best nights of her life.

Then why did her body heat when Trevor cornered her in the barn? Why did his voice, his body, his presence send a chill up her spine? She'd never been a girly-girl, and the thought of appearing weak in front of the crew she worked with put her in a near panic. If she let down one barrier to let Trevor in, they'd all come crashing down soon enough, and she had shit that needed to stay hidden.

It was better if they just went back to normal and forgot what happened. That way nobody would be hurt or inconvenienced. She certainly had no plans on being his fuck buddy. What they shared had been both difficult and beautiful for her. She never knew if she'd be able to handle being intimate with a man, and he proved that it was possible.

Jenna decided her next course of action was looking into getting more hired hands for the ranch. Focusing on business would help. She planned to ride over to the Johnston farm and ask the guys there if they knew anyone that was looking for work. If not, word spread fast.

She untied her horse from the fence post around back, mounted, and took off without looking back. The early morning sun lightly warmed her face, and the breeze was perfect, not too hot yet. She loved riding free, not a care in the world. The softly rolling open fields were a mix of golds and greens. The sight soothed her soul and calmed her anxiety.

Jenna wondered how Grace was fairing on her honeymoon, and smiled. She also wondered how Mr. Wagner would feel now that Grace and Scott would be out of his house, starting their own lives. He didn't deserve to be lonely like her. Sometimes she believed he was the only reason she could get through a day. Just a few words from him in his deep, gravelly voice, a touch or a smile, were enough to make her world brighter.

Her peripheral vision caught a glimpse of movement, and when she turned, Conner was riding horseback beside her.

"Where you going?" she shouted over the wind and the pounding of hooves.

"I want to talk to you." Conner wasn't a talker. She knew all the cowboys on the ranch well. He was the most difficult to read. All she knew was that he was a loner, living alone in a small cottage out back instead of in the trailers with the other ranch hands. He was taller and more built than most, and always had hard-set features as if pissed off with the world. She could respect a man's man. He got the job done without shooting the shit and wasting time.

As he rode alongside her in just a fitted white T-shirt and blue jeans, despite the early morning chill, she could see the edge of his black tribal tattoo peeking out from his sleeve. She'd seen him topless on a few rare occasions. He had a black patterned tattoo on each upper arm and an American flag over his heart. His nipples were pierced, which got him teased by the other cowboys at first. Until they learned that Conner had the muscle to back up his attitude. Now all the other ranch hands steered clear.

She had no clue why he'd need to speak to her. Trevor was the go-to guy, being the foreman.

Jenna slowed her horse when they reached a small patch of forest. "What is it, cowboy?"

He dismounted, walking around the front of her horse with his spurs clattering with each step. Conner leaned against a mature oak tree, his arms crossed over his chest.

She slipped off her horse and took a few steps forward. Of all men, he should know not to mess with her. When he first arrived at the ranch and hit on her, she shot a hole in the barn wall inches from his head. He minded his own business after that. Maybe he needed another lesson? Her rifle was strapped to the side of her horse, so she didn't get too close to him, just in case.

"What were you talking to Wagner about the morning of the wedding? You looked like you were crying when you came out of his office."

"You came all the way out here to talk to me for that? I have business matters to attend to."

"So you *were* crying?"

She ground her teeth. What point was he trying to make? "No, I don't cry. Ever. Happy now?"

"You're a woman. There's nothing wrong with showing emotion."

"I'm not like other women."

He dropped his bent-up leg and stepped toward her, each step ringing with that familiar metallic chime. She instinctively moved back, her heart beginning to race. She took a quick glance to her left to eye her rifle.

"You gonna shoot me?" He kept coming until she was past her horse and out of reach of her weapon. "I have a better idea."

She narrowed her gaze and gave him her most heated death stare. He only smirked, a devilish smirk, but one nonetheless. "If you lay one finger on me, I guarantee you'll go home with scrambled eggs."

"I'm onto you." Her back hit another tree, and she felted trapped like a rat. Somehow she knew the jig was up. He'd been outside the door to Wagner's office the morning of the wedding. Did he hear something that wasn't for his ears? "I know your secrets."

She tried to laugh it off. "You're nuts. What secrets?" Jenna never realized just how tall the man was. His shadow swallowed her whole. He was raw, rugged, and pure masculine strength—everything she respected in a man. But if he knew the truth, she also feared him.

"You want me to say it?"

"Whatever you think you know, you're wrong."

He shook his head, so slowly. His dark goatee and obsidian eyes gave him a sinister edge. Why was her pussy pulsing again? Why did her body associate fear with sex? She was more fucked up than she first believed.

Conner outstretched an arm and planted it against the tree, looming close enough that she could feel his warm breath. "We're more alike than you think."

"Oh?"

"We both have a past we'd rather forget." He took a breath, suddenly losing that bravado in his eyes. "Seems this town has its share of drunken fathers."

Jenna swallowed hard. She didn't like to think about her father, but he wasn't the one who kept starring in her nightmares. She worked hard to forget the rapist who lived the next ranch over. She learned how to protect herself, how to block out emotion—all because of what he did to her. "He wasn't a drunk." Perhaps knowing what he did to her was alcohol induced would give him an excuse, but he'd been sober as a priest on Sunday.

"Just stop. I heard everything you talked to Wagner about. Your father messed you up. I can understand that." He pulled back, looking down on her with a blank expression. "Hiding from the truth, pretending to be someone you're not, isn't going to change the past."

She thought for a moment. The jig was up, and she felt the fabric of her world unraveling. She'd have to go along with his theory of a drunken father damaging her. It was better than the truth. Her defenses rose in response. "You're a hypocrite then. Aren't you the one hiding from your past? You block everyone out and seclude yourself in that shack out back. I've never seen you in a real relationship. You barely maintain friendships. Is that normal?"

"It's the best I can do. You should know how it is. Being strong can protect you from getting hurt. I think we could help each other."

Jenna thought about the years since she arrived on the Wagner ranch. Being strong kept her together, but it didn't help her heal, didn't make her happy. "I don't need your help."

"Sometimes letting go of control, letting go of those barriers, can be liberating. I can show you how—"

"Stop!" Was he going to suggest what she thought he was? "You actually think I'll play your games, Conner? Don't you know me at all? If anyone's going to play the dominant, it's me. If you're looking for a beating, come find me. Otherwise, get out of my way." Heat crept out of her collar. She ducked under Conner's arm and stormed away, no fear lingering. "No man will ever hold power over me!" *Not again.*

She took short work of mounting her horse and jammed her heels to its side for a hasty retreat. It was already beginning—what she feared when arriving on the Wagner Ranch. Her secret was spreading, and the men were already after her. Conner actually expected she'd be into his BDSM shit? She clenched her teeth, wishing she had given him another warning shot for such an indecent proposal. How would she remain invisible if the ranch hands saw her as a potential bedmate? The thought of all those men, her coworkers, looking at her with that familiar lust in their eyes made her cringe. She'd have to leave, but go where? This was her home. She loved Mr. Wagner and shouldn't have to change her life.

Chapter Eight

"Fuck," Conner muttered.

He must be out of his mind to think he could have a piece of Jenna. Lesbian or not, she was untouchable. He planned to persuade her right into his bed, never thinking about rejection. When he did decide to play with a woman, they were usually agreeable. Jenna really was a lot like him, both with damaged childhoods thanks to bastard fathers. She could hide from the truth, like he did, but it didn't change the facts.

Conner knew his days of sanity were numbered. Trying to forget the daily beatings when his father would come home stinkin' drunk from the bars was impossible. The memories invaded even his dreams each night. Worse than his beatings was the fact that the motherfucker gave the same treatment to his mother. Watching the one woman he loved abused while he was too small and weak to defend her would haunt him until the day he died.

As soon as he became a man, capable of defending himself, he stood up for himself. He remembered that day, the day he confronted that drunkard. Conner had grown taller than his father, and had youth and strength on his side. He didn't beat the man, even though tempted, but stilled his fist. The fear dancing in the older man's eyes was payment enough. He warned him that day that if he ever laid a finger on his mother again, he'd kill him. He meant it. Conner left home and never looked back. He took general labor positions at various farms until settling at the Wagner Ranch.

He never touched alcohol. The smell triggered unwanted memories, and he refused to become the spitting image of his father.

Still, real relationships weren't possible for him. To shut down the memories, it was necessary to close out all emotion. A relationship would require love, something he wasn't capable of giving. What about a family? What kind of father would he make? Would history repeat itself? It was a chance he wasn't willing to make.

One thing Conner learned early on was that he had to be in control during sex. From his first encounters, it was necessary. As the years progressed, things became more extreme, to the point that he couldn't perform unless he had complete dominance over a woman. Why? Was he becoming his father, eager to abuse a woman in any way possible? No, his brand of dominance was about giving and receiving pleasure through pain and control. He didn't want the women that shared his bed to suffer. Unlike his father, he didn't believe in harming a woman.

Thinking about Jenna tied down, submissive and begging, made his cock harder than any woman was capable of. She was so alive, so strong. Dominating her would be the ultimate challenge. He knew it would be a match made in heaven, too. She played the tough cowgirl to camouflage a damaged interior. He could build her up, teach her that being the submissive could be a positive thing. As her dominant, he'd show her that he'd never hurt her, never abuse her trust. But getting such a headstrong woman to agree to participate seemed an impossible task.

He and Jenna really were alike, both closed and functional. The other ranch hands laughed and played as hard as they worked. Conner only worked. His free time was spent reflecting in his private place. Feeling sorry for himself. He felt drawn to Jenna. She wasn't about bullshit and didn't grate at his nerves like some of the greenhorns could with such little effort. He respected her. The more she pushed him away, the more he had to have her. *To own her.*

* * * *

It had been a long, hard day of working with the cattle. Trevor hadn't seen Jenna again, not until now. As the sun began to set and he prepared to call it a day, she slowed to a trot as she neared the barn. The remnants of sunlight highlighted her blonde hair, and her blue eyes bore into his once she dismounted. Her face was blank, but not ignoring him had to be a good sign.

She could play cold all she wanted. Trevor knew she had feelings for him. What they shared was mutually enjoyed. When he pinned her in the barn, he didn't fail to notice her pulse increase and her throat working harder. For some reason, she continued to deny herself, as if she had to live up to being some stone-cold bitch. He knew her secret, maybe he should have made that more clear.

Jenna led her horse to the bay doors and swatted him in. She had her horse better trained than any he'd ever seen, and it returned to its stall without delay. "So, how's the branding coming along?"

"We had a good day considering we're short-staffed. Any luck finding help?"

"I think so. The guys at the Johnston ranch are spreading the word, and a couple are gonna stop by next week." She looked preoccupied. Were they going to go back to a working relationship and pretend nothing happened between them? That may work for awhile, but he'd never be able to forget. Could she?

"You finished for the day?"

She ignored his pointless small talk. "Did Conner talk to you? Tell you anything about me?"

He thought about it. Should he play dumb or keep things honest between them? "I wouldn't have come to your place if he hadn't."

"Shit!" She spun around, raking her hands through her hair. "I knew it! You came looking for one thing. Who else knows? Don't tell me the whole ranch's been talking about it."

He remained calm. The interior of the barn was dim now, most of the ranch hands off for the night. Trevor was always the last to leave for the evening, due to his responsibility as foreman. "Nobody knows." He almost whispered as he approached her. "I don't plan on telling a soul, darlin'."

"Good. Keep it that way."

"I will. I don't plan on sharing you." Once close enough, he ducked his head and nuzzled her neck, pulling her closer with an arm around the waist. She needed to let go and admit she wanted this as much as he did.

She didn't pull away, but whispered against his hair, "Why are you doing this to me, foreman?"

"Say my name."

"No."

"Remember what I did to you with my tongue? I'll suck your sweet little pussy right here. Anything you want, say the word." He nipped her earlobe, making her shudder. *"Say my name."*

"Trevor, don't do this. I can't handle being one of your flings." Was she one of his flings? He never stayed with one woman because he either lost interest or declared himself too young to settle down. He didn't mess with women looking for a serious relationship to start with. Trevor wasn't sure what Jenna wanted, but she was far different from his other women.

"I want you so bad, sweet thing." When he pulled back, he saw her eyes closed, her lips parted. "Tell me you want my cock."

"So help me, cowboy, you better not speak one word of this to anyone." With that, she pulled off her heavy flannel shirt and unclasped her sports bra. This was a wicked fantasy that he wouldn't let slip away.

He didn't answer her, just dropped down to her luscious breasts, the ones he hadn't stopped fantasizing about. He rubbed his cheeks against the billowy fullness before suckling one of her nipples like a starved infant. It would take him a lifetime before he had his fill of Jenna. He dropped down to one knee, kissing her flat stomach. She held his head in place.

Blindly, he unbuttoned and unzipped her Levi's, and tugged them down her rounded hips. He kissed down her stomach before lapping at her clit. She nearly toppled over before suddenly stabilizing.

Jenna gasped. "What the—"

He glanced up to see a dark shadow towering behind Jenna, holding her upright. Conner's hands snaked around her and cupped her breasts. His large hands barely contained her flesh. He'd never shared a woman with Conner, but he wasn't new to ménage sex.

"You're fucking soft," Conner grated. Rather than bolt and throw a fit, Jenna leaned her head back against his chest. If she was willing to share herself, who would lead this party? Trevor was used to being the one in control, directing the action. It didn't have to be spoken that he held rank on the farm. When he'd shared Grace with three other cowboys, it was him alone that orchestrated the party. Conner wasn't your typical ranch hand. He'd never listen to a command from Trevor in a sex game. It was hard enough to get him to follow orders when they worked together.

"What am I doing?" she mumbled to herself.

"You're being a good girl," said Conner, spinning her around. "Now undo my belt and grab my cock."

Okay, the guy had balls.

* * * *

Jenna felt immersed in an erotic fog. Being so exposed in the large, open barn, Trevor teasing her with his skilled tongue, and then a new hard body behind her, was a wicked combination. She hadn't stopped thinking of Conner all day. He'd looked so damn sexy when he stopped her earlier. *Even more.* An odd bond had cemented between them because of their past experiences. She had wanted to let go and allow him to lead her into his world of naughty pleasures, but she kept her pride and ran away before she did something she'd regret.

She was already beyond resisting Trevor. It was only a matter of time until she gave in to him again after what she knew he could do to her. She craved more kisses, to feel his hard, muscled body, and reach the beautiful peak he brought her to so effortlessly.

Now both her fantasy men, the two that knew her true identity, were sharing her nude body. The multitude of sensations flowing through every inch of her flesh made her pliant and eager. She knew all about their ménage encounters, even with Grace. She'd seen the marks on the other woman's body when she'd changed and knew they were from the Wagner cowboys, but kept her mouth shut. Would they be rough with her, too? Leave marks on her flesh from their powerful lovemaking? Her pussy wept just contemplating the idea.

Her mind was a jumble. Jenna didn't want to be a number, one of their loose women. She didn't know what she wanted. Part of her craved to give in and allow these men to love her, shelter her, and never let her go. Another part insisted on remaining independent, strong, safe from any emotional attachment. It was a whirlwind of emotion playing in her head at the same time as her body was heating deliciously.

The consequences tomorrow would be substantial. Fucking two of the crew would make working the farm nearly impossible. They wouldn't be able to keep their mouths shut, and soon every cowboy would be after her. But right now all she could do was comply. She unbuckled Conner and reached in his boxers. His cock was already fully erect, hard, and almost hot. She wrapped her hand around his length, her fingers unable to meet. If she thought Trevor was huge, this guy was too big to be holy. Jenna anticipated him penetrating her with both apprehension and excitement.

"Now I want your mouth around me. Get on your knees."

She obeyed like a robot, not because he commanded it, but because she desperately needed to taste him. What would a real man taste like? Conner was all male, and his deep voice giving her orders sent a violent thrill through her that had her pussy pulsing in deep, desperate waves. His aura was all dominance and confidence, lulling her into submission.

Jenna bent down to her knees and tested his cock with the tip of her tongue. She wasn't sure what to do, but acted on impulse. His cock was soft like silk on her tongue but hard and unforgiving as she took several inches into her mouth.

"Suck it," Conner commanded. "Deeper."

She did as ordered, sucking his cock. As she took more of his impossible length down her throat, she began to gag as his cock filled her mouth, and she had to pull away.

"Did I tell you to stop? If you want this to work, you have to do as you're told."

He stroked his cock, which fascinated her, calming her irritation at his comment. She wasn't used to doing as she was told. The idea of giving up control and trusting another person to not hurt her was tempting. Deep down, she knew she needed to hand over power to eliminate the fears caused by her rapist. He had stolen her control without permission. He took her innocence in a brutal way—along with it her trust, her security, everything pure within her.

"It's too big to suck," she said.

Conner grabbed both her upper arms and tugged her up against his chest, looking down on her. "We should set some ground rules." He gave her a firm squeeze as if warning her to obey. She almost laughed, but played along. "Do as you're told, don't ask questions, and I guarantee you'll have the best night of your life."

She nodded.

"Say, yes, master." His dark eyes were black orbs in the dim interior of the barn.

"Fuck you." She twisted out of his grip, landing in Trevor's embrace. He'd taken off his shirt, and his skin against hers sizzled against her bare breasts. "I'm not doing this, Trevor!"

Conner had to be out of his mind. *Master?* That would be the day. She was slave to no man. The only master of her body was her. The mere idea of lowering herself to boost some deranged cowboy's ego was bullshit.

"Give it a try, darlin'. You never know unless you try." Trevor, too? She was outnumbered and wondering why she agreed to this sex party at all.

"You want me to call him master? Is that how you think of me?" Jenna tugged her jeans up and covered her breasts with crossed arms as her lusty haze lifted.

Conner's deep voice slithered up her spine like phantom fingertips. "There's nothing wrong with submitting, Jenna. It can be liberating. You'll learn to enjoy it." He pulled the elastic from her hair, which then fanned down over her back in a soft sweep. "It's not about control. It's about trust, letting go."

She exhaled and refocused. Maybe she was being too hasty. There was a growing portion of the population that was into BDSM, so it couldn't be all bad. Her friend Kylie, who worked in town, had been in such a relationship in the past and had enjoyed it, tempted to return to the lifestyle even after the breakup. Conner was all male. If dominance had a face, it was his. But she was no wilting flower—she ate cowboys for breakfast and sent them running for cover when they pissed her off.

"Not a word," she said.

"Of course not. This is between the three of us," Conner promised. Then he hoisted her up into his arms as if she weighed ten pounds. He carried her to the branding table, a thick slab of solid wood, and set her on it. She wiggled back, her legs dangling over the edge at the knees. The breeze sweeping in from the open bay doors was still warm, but had a hint of evening chill which made her nipples pebble. The remnants of daylight faded quickly. Her eyes had difficulty adjusting, and she couldn't monitor the movements of both men. The landscape beyond the barn was a black void closing in on them.

The strike of a match caught her attention. She watched as Trevor lit an oil lantern, which offered a warm glow to a small bubble of space. The lines and curves of his body were accentuated by shadows. He returned to her, standing between her legs and spreading her arms wide. His hands were like shackles around her wrists.

"You look gorgeous, darlin'." Trevor kissed her temple and trailed kisses along her jawline. She closed her eyes as his soft lips calmed her. He radiated a quiet energy that pulled down her barriers.

She wanted to reach up and smooth her hands over his shoulders, but he continued to hold her still. Conner chucked his shirt. His body was brutally masculine, making her folds moisten. The lamplight glimmered off the little silver loops through his nipples. Her curiosity was piqued.

"You like?" Conner moved to her side. She had the overwhelming urge to tongue-play with those hoops. His chest was chiseled, and those tats made him a forbidden fruit she had to taste.

She nodded.

"Let her touch me." Trevor complied and released her wrists. She didn't hesitate to bring her hands up, landing one palm on Trevor's broad shoulder, the other over Conner's hard pec. Her eyes lolled back in her head as their masculine heat invaded her, making her lust-drunk and hungry. She ran her hands over their smooth, warm flesh. They stood solid, like unmovable mountains. These two strong cowboys were controlling her, possessing her—but she had power, too. She chose to play along and knew they were as desperate to fuck her as she was to feel them filling her.

"I'm going to suck your pussy, but you're not allowed to come. Understand?"

Again, keeping her promise to stay quiet, she nodded. Her entire body tingled as she anticipated what Conner had planned for her.

"Lean back." He spread her legs as she dropped down to her back over the thick wooden utility table. Trevor was beside her now, painting a trail along her collarbone with his tongue. When he latched on to her sensitive breast, she arched up. Conner was in position and clamped down over her cunt. She moaned, not even attempting to hold back. Tonight was about her deepest, darkest fantasies. About letting go. Conner ate her as if she were his last meal, more intense than Trevor had been. He wouldn't allow her a respite, and she felt an overwhelming buildup of erotic pressure that she couldn't handle. His goatee brushed her sensitive folds with a mix of pain and pleasure. If he didn't stop, her body would explode against his wish, and for some reason she wanted to do as she was told, wanted him to approve and be proud of her.

"I can't…" How did he expect her to hang on when he was so damn good with his tongue? She grabbed Trevor's bicep and squeezed. With her other hand she fisted her hand into Conner's hair, willing him to let her breathe for just a second.

When he pulled up, his eyes were glazed over. A feral look flitted through his gaze, and her breathing hitched. God, she wanted him to punish her, to bring her into his world, the one she saw when he looked at her with such intensity.

"You cold, darlin'?" asked Trevor, pulling her back into a sitting position. She shook her head, still unwilling and unable to speak. Conner had brought her to the very edge and left her hanging. Her body was hot-wired and ripe.

Chapter Nine

Conner felt the beast clawing to get out and knew he had to rein it in. He didn't want to scare Jenna off when they just got started. The fact she agreed at all was beyond his expectations. He'd never shared a woman before because control was everything to him. If he had to include another man, it would be Trevor. They shared Jenna's secret, and he respected Trevor more than the other ranch hands. On the fields, they worked well as a team, getting the job done with little verbal communication, both sensing the other's actions before they made a move. The greenhorns these days didn't have the same work ethic.

"I need to see her tied down to this table," said Conner. He didn't have to say more. Trevor stepped away to collect a coil of thin yellow rope. Conner removed his boots and pants. He helped Jenna to her back and spread her legs. Her pussy was swollen and moist, and he couldn't wait to get inside her.

Trevor pulled her arms straight above her head, her breasts stretching out temptingly. He secured her wrists as if he'd done this before. Conner raised an eyebrow, but Trevor only winked and continued binding Jenna to the slab of wood.

Conner bound her by the knees, rather than the ankles. He wanted her stretched wide and fully exposed. Being in the open barn, rather than his private cabin, added to the sex appeal of what they were doing. Jenna, tied down and submissive, was his ultimate fantasy. "You ready for my cock? I'm liable to break a little thing like you."

"I don't care." She writhed, arching her pelvis up and tugging at her binds.

With her cunt at the edge of the table, he stood between her legs. Even in the dim lighting, her pussy glistened. He pressed the tip of his cock at her entrance, unsure if he'd be able to fuck her without hurting her. When she winced, he pulled back. "Trev, where's that trunk of yours?"

He knew Trevor and his lackeys had a treasure trove of sex toys hidden somewhere in the barn. "I'll grab it." Trevor bounded off into the dark interior of the barn.

"Just you and me for a minute, Jenna." Conner leaned over and laid one kiss over her clit. Then he trailed individual kisses up her stomach toward her breasts. Never had he been with such a full-bosomed woman. He massaged her tits, watching her squirm. When her eyes rolled closed, he pinched her nipples, hard. Her eyes shot open as she gasped. "You like that?"

"No. You're hurting me!" She pulled too hard at the rope around her wrists.

"You like it. Now, stop struggling or you'll rub your wrists raw." He wasn't an asshole. He just knew his women well, and that look in her eyes told him all he needed to know. There was a fine line between sexual pleasure and pain. She'd learn in a hurry that there was nothing better, and soon she'd beg him to take her into that zone.

He pinched her again. This time her gasp ended with a moan. She scowled at him when he smirked. "You better not hurt me, Conner." He knew she spoke about abusing her trust, not her body.

Against his better judgment, he leaned over and kissed her on the lips. He usually didn't kiss on the lips. If he did, it wasn't face-to-face like he was with Jenna. This felt intimate, personal, and new. She kissed him back as if starved for attention, and he soon lost himself to her. He even closed his eyes and focused on the feel of her plump, pink lips, her lively tongue, and sweet taste. Before he realized how much time had passed, Trevor clapped him on the back.

Conner felt as if he were caught exposed and vulnerable because for those few minutes, he let everything go and savored the woman under him. He wasn't sure what to think, or feel.

"This what you wanted?" Trevor held out a tube of lube. Conner snatched it and poured a healthy dose in his palm. As he smoothed the sticky substance up and down his rigid cock, he held eye contact with Jenna. Was she as affected by their kiss?

He slipped a hand under her ass as he positioned his lubed dick with the other. Pushing in an inch at a time was excruciating when he wanted to take her hard and fast. Conner wasn't used to denying himself anything, especially during sex.

"You're too big," she whined, her breathing coming in rapid gasps.

"Hush." He continued to push in, slowly filling her. Her pussy clamped impossibly tight around his dick, nearly making him come before he started.

"Relax, darlin'," said Trevor, brushing stray hairs from her forehead. He dipped his hand down her body and teased her clit. Conner didn't brush him away—he wanted Jenna to enjoy herself, and Trevor knew how to make her relax. There may be something to sharing after all. They seemed to work together with a woman as easily as they did in the fields.

Jenna began to make sexy mewling sounds, licking her lips and tightening around his cock. "She wants to suck something, Trev." The men shared a wicked glance. Trevor climbed the solid table and straddled Jenna's chest.

* * * *

Trevor couldn't wait to feel Jenna's sweet lips around his throbbing erection. When he watched her suck Conner, he only imagined taking his place. He looked down on Jenna, her arms straight above her head. She'd never get free from one of his knots.

When she licked her lips, he thought he'd lose it. "You're not gonna bite me, are you, sweet thing?"

"I thought cowboys weren't afraid of anything." She licked her lips, and he couldn't wait another second. Her mouth opened in a gasp as Conner pushed into her pussy from behind him. He used the opportunity to feed her his cock. Holding the base of his shaft, she clamped down around him, sucking greedily. Every time Conner thrust, she sucked harder, expelling her energy on his dick. He dropped forward, bracing his weight on his arms as he fucked her mouth.

He lost track of time when Conner's gruff voice suddenly commanded Jenna. "Come!" She tugged Trevor's dick side to side in her mouth as she writhed on the wooden table. Any minute and she'd explode as she had in her apartment last night with him. His balls tightened as she continued to suckle him. "Jenna. Come!"

She released her latch on his cock and called out as tremors wracked her body. It was the sweetest sound he'd ever heard. Conner groaned behind him. Trevor began to fist his shaft, desperate for release. Jenna's body seemed to melt once Conner pulled out of her body. She watched him through hooded eyes as he straddled her, masturbating quick and hard. He tossed his head back as the pressure built up, taking him to that perfect pre-orgasmic realm. When he erupted, he watched as a strong arch of white ejaculate sprayed over Jenna's breasts and neck. It was the sexiest thing he'd ever seen, but he also worried she'd kill him for defiling her.

"You okay?" he asked. Her breathing appeared steadier now. He slipped off the table and noted Conner already untying her legs. Trevor did the same for her arms. As soon as she was free, he pulled her into his arms and held her. "Darlin', answer me."

"I'm fine." She rubbed her wrists, but he took them in his hands and kissed them.

"I'm taking her back to my place to wash her up." Conner already had his jeans and boots back on. "I'll see you at sunrise."

Trevor didn't want to leave her, didn't want to hand her over to another man. But the two shared a brief look, one that said they needed this time alone together. Trevor wasn't married to the woman. This was just some hard-core playing. He didn't have the right to lay claim to her. "See you in the mornin'." He kissed Jenna on the forehead before she was whisked out of his arms by Conner.

They disappeared into the cool night air, consumed by darkness as soon as they crossed the threshold of the bay doors. Trevor grabbed a clean rag hanging over the nearest stall and cleaned himself before redressing. His cock was still semi-firm. He wanted to double fuck Jenna, to feel her tight, virgin ass grip him until he reached his peak inside her. But tonight crossed enough barriers. She'd need time before accepting two cocks at the same time.

He held his shirt in one hand as he made his way back to the trailer. If he was expected to be alert for the last day of branding, he needed rest. If he could get Jenna off his mind, maybe he'd get some much-needed sleep.

"You're out late." He nearly jumped out of his skin when the girl appeared from the corner of the barn.

"Brittany? What are you still doing here?"

It was too dark to make out her features, or what she wore. Instead, her hands landed on his bare chest. "Our mother wanted to stay an extra week. Apparently she likes it here."

"It is a beautiful piece of land."

"It's boring."

His first reaction was to tell her that he could keep her boredom at bay. Any other time, he'd usher her back to the trailer, or to the tack room, and fuck her until she begged him to stop. This time, he said nothing. He realized that Jenna was branded on his brain, and he couldn't shake the feeling that he was dishonoring her by being with another woman. What was wrong with him? He'd always been carefree when it came to sex. It's how he lived.

"Cowboy? I'm cold. Aren't you going to warm me up?"

The idea of intimacy with Brittany felt wrong. Somehow Jenna had claimed him. Was it the mark on his neck, or had she worked her way to his heart? Whatever it was, he wouldn't bed another woman when all he could envision was Jenna's baby blue eyes.

"I'll show you back to the house. Wagner usually has a fire going this time of night." With a hand to her back, he navigated them through the dark backyard to the main house. She had her arms crossed over her chest, like a sullen child when the spotlights highlighted their forms.

"Thanks for nothing." Brittany slammed the patio doors to the kitchen shut behind her, leaving him alone with his confused thoughts and the long walk back to his trailer.

Chapter Ten

Jenna sat on the edge of Conner's large bed and used the damp cloth he gave her to clean her chest. She'd never spent time in his cabin, only popped in every once in awhile with clean linen. It was small, but tidy. Simplistic. Conner was anything but simple. She wanted to know everything about him. Part of her had claimed both men as they each claimed her body. Were they even capable of committing? Was she even capable of love?

"So this is where you hide out." Jenna looked around the room. It was just one room with wood plank walls and a single window. No need for a kitchen since all the men had their meals at the main house. There was a long dresser and mirror, a blanket box, and a night-side table. An old, worn, brown leather chair sat in the far corner. She imagined him spending countless hours in that chair, staring at the walls and reflecting on memories better left forgotten. So much like her.

"I'm not good with people."

She studied his back, the muscles flexing as he rummaged through his drawers. "You seem to get along well with Trevor." He'd easily shared her with the other man, but without an emotional attachment to her, it wouldn't be that hard. Just another fuck.

"No more talking." He turned around and held some sort of rubber sex toy in his hand. Her pussy clenched, and her heart rate picked up. Could she handle what he dished out? She wasn't so sure now that she was alone with him.

"Shall I call you master now?" She scoffed and tugged up the blanket to cover her breasts.

"How about 'big daddy' then?" Jenna cringed.

He tossed the toy on the bed and sat down beside her. Although he always looked ready to kill, she rarely saw him flustered, and he never raised his voice...He was an enigma. "I know about your father. Forget him. I'm your daddy now, understand?" Did she actually hear concern in his voice? Could it be that simple—allowing Conner to replace the wicked men from her past?

"Conner, don't go there. You don't know the half of it."

"That's the past. I'm here now. Nobody's going to hurt you again because you have me."

He was close enough to feel the warmth radiating from his bare skin. Conner was a tall man, all sinewy muscle and broad shoulders. Nobody ever spoke gently to her, always treating her as she portrayed herself—tough and cold. She felt tears pricking at the backs of her eyes, but she didn't do tears. What was happening to her? "I have you tonight. Tomorrow's another story."

He scowled. "Lie down."

Why the fuck not? She'd already crossed too many personal barriers to fathom. She dropped to her back with an exhale. There was no fight left in her.

"You're beautiful. You know that, right?"

"You're not so bad yourself." She offered a smile. Conner wasn't one to give compliments, and she appreciated it, for what it was worth.

He ran a finger down her inner thigh, making her shiver. "I'm going to teach you to trust me, Jenna."

"You've got your work cut out for you, cowboy. I don't do trust."

"That's why I have to teach you." He parted her legs, standing directly in front of her prone body. Conner stared down at her with a blank face—no lust, no hunger, no love or hate. She felt her nerves rising under his scrutinizing gaze. When she reached for the sheet to cover herself, he shook his head slowly, so she dropped her hand. He had such a dominant energy that even she felt compelled to obey.

He took a deep breath and opened the drawer to his night-side table, and then reached for the toy lying beside her. She watched in fascination as he drizzled the clear lube onto the red rubber toy.

"What do you plan on doing with that thing?"

"Do you know what it is?" He held it out for her visual inspection. She shook her head. It was too small to be a dildo.

"It's a butt plug." Conner licked his lips, looking down on her with a new feral need. "Have you ever been fucked up the ass?"

"Hell no!" She shifted up to lean on her elbows.

He scowled, his eyes darkening. "I guess I should have warned you. When you refuse to listen, you get punished."

As much as she wanted to kick him in the nuts and bolt from the cabin, her curiosity was also piqued—and the man looked so goddamn sexy standing there in just his faded blue jeans. What would it feel like to trail her tongue over his chest, down his ripped abs? She wanted to feel his nipple rings as she sucked them. Besides, she was a big girl, and not often afraid of physical pain.

She resigned. "Do your worst, cowboy." She may have agreed to play along, but he didn't intimidate her.

Before she knew what was happening, he'd twisted her around to her stomach and hoisted her further up on the bed so he could straddle the backs of her legs. She tried to push up on her arms, but a strong hand forced her back down to the mattress.

"Three should be enough for a first offense, don't you think?" She wasn't sure what he was talking about until his palm came down hard on her ass. Jenna screeched and twisted in an attempt to dish out the same punishment to Conner, but again, he held her in place. Another spank, and then another. The guy had big hands, just as he had a big dick to match. Her ass cheek throbbed, but for some reason her clit had been sent into overdrive and now pulsed to a desperate beat. She wanted more, but wouldn't dare ask and show weakness.

"Now we can get somewhere." Conner spread her ass cheeks apart, and the cool jolt of the lubed toy hit her puckered hole. She clenched down hard in an attempt to resist his invasion.

"Stick that thing up your own ass!"

"This will be much easier if you relax. But if you want it hard and fast, I have no problem with it. You'll be the one with the sore ass."

He had a point. This was going to happen, so she may as well get the most out of the experience. Jenna realized her ass was a virgin, untouched. She didn't want another painful memory, but a good one, good enough to help her forget the other.

She took measured breaths and loosened her muscles. She wanted to tell him she was afraid, that this was all so new to her, but sharing her feelings felt too foreign. Instead, she braced herself as he twisted the toy into her impossibly tight opening. He didn't use force, but slow, measured movements. When it lodged snuggly, he rolled her to her back so he straddled her waist. "It feels weird," she said.

"It'll feel much better soon enough. I just need to loosen you up so I can share you properly tomorrow."

More than a night? "You're gonna share me with Trevor?" she asked, disbelief ringing in her words.

"He likes you. If I try and keep you for myself, there'll be a shit storm to pay."

Her mind reeled. Trevor and Conner acted as if these sex games were going to continue long-term. Did they plan to keep her as the ranch whore, to be used as needed? No way in hell would that happen. She'd given herself to Trevor when she was at an emotional low. After he taught her the pleasures of the flesh, she had willingly allowed Conner to join them, only because she'd harbored secret desires for both men for years.

"Now for those pretty little nipples." He drew two pink clips from his jean pocket.

"Nope. Uh-uh." She fought him now, not willing to have him torture her breasts. Jenna managed to land several sharp blows to his chest before he shackled her wrists by the sides of her head. She felt vulnerable without a weapon, but it also felt liberating to hand over power. He had said this was about trust, but trust was the hardest thing to give over.

He dipped his head and sucked her tit, his goatee grazing her sensitive flesh. As pressure rose in her cunt, she clenched around the rubber toy and gasped at the thrill that spiraled through the length of her body. "That's a girl. Now you're getting it."

"But I was naughty. Aren't you gonna spank me again?" *Please spank me.*

His chuckle was dark and sinful. This cowboy was sex on a stick, and she wanted everything he had to dish out. "Only if you call me, *Big Daddy.*"

That was a difficult one, but so necessary. The past needed to stay where it belonged. Jenna was a strong, independent woman. She shouldn't be a prisoner to her nightmares—she was better than that.

"Spank me, Big Daddy." She swallowed hard. Once the words came out, the floodgates of her desire were unleashed.

"Say please."

"Fucking spank me!" She tugged her hands, still locked in place against the mattress by his strong hold. He looked at her with a twisted desire. She preferred this over the blank slate—at least he could feel something.

He shifted until he had both her wrists in one hand and nearly dragged her body to the edge of the bed as he stood up beside it, like a primitive man and his mate. With a firm hold on her, he dipped his free hand under the bed and came up with a length of rope. "Hold still," he said as he stretched her arms up toward the wooden headboard. "You sure you wanna get spanked again? You may just regret that decision."

Conner wasn't gentle, but didn't hurt her either. She enjoyed this rough side of him. Jenna may be petite, but she worked as hard as any of the men on the ranch. She craved Conner's brutality, his rough and dirty cowboy handling.

Once secured, he rolled her to her side and smacked her ass. Hard. She yelped, and then begged for more. Jenna promised herself not to beg, but she needed this so damn badly. Her body had heated to such a degree, that if he released her, she'd wrestle him down just to get a feel, a taste.

He wiggled the toy in her ass, sending an illicit jolt through her body—followed by a solid smack to her ass cheek. Conner continued the sequence until she was moaning. The meaty sound of flesh meeting flesh filled the small room.

"Had enough?"

She narrowed her eyes, tugging at her binds. "Untie me."

He shook his head, so she attempted to kick him. Her mind and body battled with a violent mix of desire and aggression. She wanted to hurt and fuck, even sink her teeth into his thick muscles. Conner easily grabbed her calf and kissed her ankle teasingly before tossing her limb back on the bed unceremoniously. He kicked off his pants, leaving her in awe at the size of his monster cock. *She'd actually had that inside her earlier.*

"You're being a bad girl, Jenna. Maybe I shouldn't give you my cock."

If he denied her with her body this pent up, she was sure she'd die. "Fuck you, Conner. Get your ass on this bed!"

"You don't understand how this works, do you?" He knelt on the bed, his cock jutting out like a virile arrow. She attempted to kick him again, so he pinned her legs between his as he straddled her. "I'm in control."

She bit her tongue. He could say whatever he wanted now because she wouldn't be restrained forever. Conner leaned forward and collected her breasts in his hands. His hot mouth covered one of her nipples and sucked. "God, yes!" She was starved for stimulation at this point. Her ass continually convulsed around the evil phallus, nearly bringing her to orgasm.

"If I untie you, will you be a good girl for your Big Daddy?"

"Untie me."

"Don't fuck with me or I'll spank your ass until it's red as a branding iron." He leaned up to unfasten the rope holding her arms above her head. The moment she was free, she lunged to a sitting position and gripped his shoulders. She did a quick visual sweep of his body, so close. Those nipple rings and tats had a direct effect on her hormone level.

"Your ink…"

He glanced at his upper arm. "What about my ink?"

She bit her lower lip as her stomach cramped with need. "I wanna taste."

* * * *

Conner wasn't used to allowing women to have their way with him. He gave the orders, and they followed willingly. Still, he couldn't deny Jenna. The thought of her lips grazing the flag on his chest or demons on his arms made his cock pulse and thicken.

"Then taste."

She started at his shoulder, tasting and nipping, moving down his muscled arm. Her tongue painted a hot trail along his tat. He'd gotten those after he left home for the last time, after he faced off with his father. They were symbolic of the demons that plagued his thoughts. If he could give them residence on his body, maybe they'd leave his head—no such luck.

"You don't scare me," she whispered as she moved to his pec. Her mouth covered his metal piercing. He closed his eyes and hissed through his teeth.

"I should."

She tugged on his jewelry with her teeth, making him wince at the combination of pleasure and pain. "I'm free now. You should be the one afraid." Jenna smirked and pushed him down to his back, her naked body straddling him in the exchange of positions. Damn, she was beautiful and sexier than sin. Her blonde hair fell over her shoulders in a soft veil, her skin soft and milky white. A fucking angel, and what was he—a devil? Just looking at her made him more aware of his budding feelings. He wanted her, to own her, possess her. Some force deep within him demanded he protect her, to show her that he wouldn't harm her like his father did his mother. Would he disappoint himself—did he dare to enter a relationship with his history? Sons were destined to commit the sins of their fathers.

After tonight she'd want nothing to do with him anyway. One night with Conner and women ran away faster than they rushed into his arms to start with. He was called sadistic, a heartless bastard—both true, he supposed. Not once had he cared about the women that shared his bed. They were there for one reason—they had a sexual appetite or a curiosity for what he did in his little forbidden cabin. Even Grace had dared to find him, and he'd given her what she sought. But, like all the others, she was gone before he woke in the morning. Who was using who?

"I'm gonna brand your ass now." He tossed her off him, ready to give her another spanking, this time over his lap so he could play with her clit. But she fought him, like a she-wolf. Struggling, twisting, and wrestling him on the bed. He could snap her in two any time he chose, but he actually enjoyed this game of hers. She liked it rough. Maybe he'd met his match, the one woman that could handle him, tame him.

The little spitfire bit him and scratched as she struggled to free herself from his grip, using all her strength and not holding back. Her breathing was ragged as they toppled over each other in a vicious, erotic dance, both naked and pumped up on adrenaline. "You're lucky I don't have my rifle, cowboy."

He pinned her on her stomach with her hands secured behind her back. Conner bent over and bit her ass. She managed to use the heel of her foot to crack a blow to his head, and the wrestling match was on again. He was tiring, and more than ready to fuck her sweet little pussy. Play time was over.

Conner used the weight of his body against hers, protecting himself from her hands and nails by intertwining his fingers with hers. Only after did he realize the intimacy of the act, especially when they were face to face, eye to eye.

"Won't you kiss me?" she asked, still panting hard.

He didn't do kissing. He'd tried it with her in the barn and lost all composure. "No kissing."

She stole from him, reaching up to capture his lips. The contact turned a switch on inside him, and he couldn't pull away like he should. He kissed her back, savoring the soft fullness of her lips, the delicate, feminine mewling sounds she made as she opened for him. He took the invitation and explored her mouth with his tongue until he was lost. Every muscle in his body went pliant, his fierce barrier lowered. He shifted slightly to the side to take some weight off her body and cupped her face with one hand. He'd never shared such a powerful bond with anyone. It only cemented the fact that he couldn't lose her, not after giving her this piece of himself. Then again, love was supposed to hurt, wasn't it? It had never been soft and sweet for him. As a child, nothing he did had ever pleased his father, and his mother carved out his heart every time she allowed herself to be victimized.

He wanted to blurt out that he loved her, like some lovesick fool. Instead, he positioned himself between her legs and thrust into her moist cunt. Her body hugged him like a tight glove. He pulled back and thrust back in, coating himself, priming her for his full invasion.

"Conner!" She arched up with a moan and grabbed the back of his neck with both hands, pulling him back to her mouth. Kissing during sex? She wrapped her legs around him in a tight embrace, forcing him to slow his movements.

They were making love. She wasn't tied down or being dominated. They were just a woman and a man, enjoying each other intimately. He pumped in and out of her body in languid strokes, brushing hair from her face and kissing her eyes, her nose. *Mine.*

Chapter Eleven

The sunlight cut a line across Jenna's face. She shifted in the bed, her body pleasantly sore. Conner's warm body was under her arm, asleep. She leaned up on her elbows and watched the gentle rise and fall of his chest. There were no harsh lines on his face. Jenna ran a fingertip along his jawline, smiling to herself. Something happened between them last night, something monumental. Trevor and Conner were now hers, marked on her soul. It was still left to be seen if they'd forget her, or if they only wanted her body and nothing more. But she saw an alternate future for herself now, one that included love and forgiveness. Would they want her if they knew her other secret? She pulled away and sat up, the sheet slipping down to her lap. The common twist of disgust churned in her gut. No way could she tell them, even if the truth ate her alive.

She flicked the little loop on his nipple playfully. They'd slept in, and there was work to be done on the ranch. No more reflection.

Conner licked his lips and squinted open his eyes. He looked shocked to see her, as if she were a ghost or a nightmare that shouldn't exist.

"You're still here."

"Where else would I be?"

"I thought you'd leave in the night." His face remained calm, a sleepy boyish quality that she could get used to waking up beside. "I've never woken up with a woman."

"Really? That's surprising." Conner wasn't a playboy like Trevor had been over the years, but he took his fair share of women to this exact bed. A possessive fire flared inside her. *No more.* She didn't want to share her men. If they were only using her, it would kill her to watch them bring girls back to the ranch or disappear into town on their weekends off. But as much as she'd like to, she wouldn't scare off the women with her rifle. Conner and Trevor were free to do as they pleased. She couldn't force them to love her any more than she could change the past.

"Seems that after a night with me, I scare them off."

"Good thing I don't scare easily." In fact, she wanted more of his punishment—more teasing, more spanks, more dominant orders that made her pussy pulse. She kissed him on the lips, just once. "Get up, cowboy. A busy day awaits you." Jenna would love to spend the day with him, learning about the man under the tough exterior, and sharing more wild romps. But, like she told him, there was work to be done.

After dressing, she slipped out of the cabin, hoping no ranch hand would spot her. She took the long way to the main house. Compared to the night of Grace's wedding, she felt so much lighter, hopeful. Conner and Trevor helped ease her burden by making sex enjoyable, something to share, rather than a weapon. She had butterflies in her stomach just thinking about seeing Trevor again.

She entered the kitchen to find Pete cleaning up from the last breakfast run. He refused to let Mr. Wagner hire a helper for him, insisting he could handle everything in the kitchen from preparation to cleanup.

"You're late. That's not like you, Jenna." Pete scrubbed down the griddle, only glancing at her from the corner of his eye. Jenna and Pete were like two peas in a pod.

"I had a busy night. I'm not hungry though, just looking for Mr. Wagner."

"He's reading the paper in the other room." He dropped his dish sponge and wiped his hands on his apron while turning around. "Something wrong?"

She denied anything was wrong, even though Pete had a sixth sense about these things. Everything was great—too great. It was bound to blow up in her face.

Mr. Wagner was on the sofa in front of the fire. She came up silently behind him, walking on the assortment of area rugs, watching the flames lick the cord of wood in the fireplace. The warmth was enough to ward off the morning chill in the open concept living room.

Her boss read a paper, sitting back casually in his flannel and blue jeans. "Not polite to sneak up on a man."

She rubbed his shoulders briefly before joining him on the sofa. "How are things going with Ms. Scarlett?"

"Wonderful. She's gone off to town with Brittany. Apparently girls need to shop as much as they need air to breathe."

"Ah. You've been spending a lot of time with her. Anything I should know?"

He folded his paper neatly and set it on the arm of the sofa. Mr. Wagner twisted slightly to face her. "She's a good friend. What about you, darlin'? My foreman can't keep the smile off his face these days. I think you're the one to blame."

"Why would you think that?"

"Because I see the same twinkle in your eyes that I see in his. It's something I haven't seen in either of you since coming to the ranch."

She shifted closer when he opened his arms in invitation. "I'm confused." Leaning into him always felt like the most natural thing in the world to do. He was her rock, her savior. "Conner found out about my secret and told Trevor. One thing led to another, and now I think I have feelings for both of them."

"Love triangles can be complicated, but not necessarily destined to failure."

A love triangle? That didn't sound good at all. They'd both shared her, but that was lust, a moment of passion. What man in his right mind would refuse a naked woman after a long day of work?

"I'm scared. This is Conner and Trevor we're talking about here. They aren't the commitment type. I'd be the first to admit that they're no-good womanizers. What was I thinking?"

"You can't help who you fall in love with. I'm sure Grace didn't come here expecting to find love, but she found it with Scott. Now look at them—married and ready to spend the rest of their lives committed to each other."

"Scott's like you." She wanted to say Trevor and Conner would take after their own drunken fathers, but bit her tongue. "They're different."

He ran his hand up and down her back as she sank against him, breathing in the comforting scent of his musky cologne. It was amazing how a scent could trigger so many emotions and memories. "Not so different. You're like a daughter to me, Trevor like a son. I want the best for the both of you." He chuckled, a deep, rich sound. "If anyone can handle those two cowboys, it's you, darlin'. They're green broke. I think they need a strong woman to tame them proper."

"I just don't want to get hurt." She fiddled with the buttons on his shirt. Mr. Wagner was the only human on Earth she dared to confide in.

"If someone has a problem with one of the cowboys, what do I tell 'em?"

She thought for a moment, and then smiled up at him. "You tell them that Jenna'll handle them."

"That's a girl. If you love those two men, claim them and make sure they know how you feel."

She stayed wrapped in his arms, enjoying the crackle of the fire for awhile longer. Love? Was it love? Real love? "How do you know when you're in love?" she whispered.

"If you're asking me, I think you already know." He kissed her atop the head before slowly walking down the hall to the kitchen to talk with Pete. She sat there alone, reflecting. Yes, she loved them. Trevor was a close friend, a good-spirited cowboy that she respected.

Conner was all male, hard-working and no nonsense. She'd just been so busy building barriers over the years that she let herself slip into the shadows.

* * * *

Even getting nearly no sleep the night before, tossing and turning in bed, Trevor was up at sunrise ready to work. He had ridden half a mile out into the open fields with his thermos of coffee after his morning shower. Watching the sunrise was worth the effort. It started by transforming the black sky to navy blue, then, as the sun rose, the colors appeared. Like magic, or some divine artist's brush, the sun emerged from its hiding place beyond the horizon and gifted him with the beautiful sight. He loved this land. Loved working it and appreciated every acre.

But there had to be more than just work and love for the land. He was a man, and one day he would need to settle down and start a family. He'd admit that he gave it all little thought, but now that Jenna had entered his life as more than just a friend and coworker, he had to reevaluate everything. She had secrets. He knew that. But she'd softened for him, let him under her tough skin, and he liked everything he found. He was determined to win her heart. Jenna was the one woman he was willing to change his ways for.

He finally found a woman he could actually give his heart to, and he had to share with another man. Of all the men on the ranch, why not Conner? Trevor was close with most of the ranch hands, but he'd developed a special bond with Conner ever since they went to the city together to find Grace. They shared a hotel for a few nights, reminiscing about their travels in life. They weren't much different from each other, both coming from abusive homes and alcoholic fathers. The difference between them was how they handled their lot in adulthood. Trevor felt he did well at moving on from the past, choosing to start fresh when he arrived on the Wagner Ranch. Conner took everything internally, breeding hate and barriers.

Jenna was the perfect woman for both of them. She knew where they were coming from because she also had a damaged past. She also wouldn't put up with any of their bullshit, which was refreshing. He knew it would take a hard-core cowgirl to get him to submit. Before returning to the barn, he headed to the front gates of the property to check the mail. As he passed the house, he saw several cowboys entering the kitchen for the first breakfast run, laughing and pushing one another. The pickup trucks were parked in the front yard of the house, soon to be off getting shipments or used to run errands. What didn't belong was the white pickup under the Wagner Ranch arch.

He stopped his horse by the driver's side door. The last person he expected to find was Steve, one of the greenhorns that tried to attack Jenna the night before the wedding. Trevor adjusted his cowboy hat as he steadied the horse with his free hand. "You have business here?" he asked.

"Trevor. Come on, you've gotta give me a break. I need this job. All the other ranchers in the area have their hired hands for the season. Could you talk to Mr. Wagner and ask him to give me another chance?"

"Mr. Wagner doesn't do the hiring. I do."

Steve ran a hand through his hair and took a breath. "You can't believe what Jenna said. I was drunk. I didn't know what I was doing. She's just overreacting."

"You put your hands on her. If Conner hadn't shown up, what were your plans?"

"I was just playing. You know I'd never actually do anything."

No, he didn't know. Trevor wanted to dismount, pull the kid from the truck, and beat him senseless. He looked at him through a cloud of red, only remembering how another man dared to touch his woman. Trevor's horse began to dance, sensing his irritation. He had to remain professional, rein back his anger.

"You're not welcome here, Steve. Get off the property, and don't come back. We don't need anyone we can't trust."

Steve's sad puppy dog face transformed into a sinister scowl as he revved his engine and scattered gravel as he barreled off the property. Trevor had a feeling he'd see that kid again.

He proceeded to get the mail pouch and headed back to the house. Mr. Wagner was sitting on the front porch in the old wooden rocking chair, one of the cow dogs obediently lying a foot away.

"You're up bright and early," said Trevor as he landed on two booted feet. He carried the mail pouch to the porch and dropped it beside Mr. Wagner.

"Just enjoying the morning, watching everything come to life."

Trevor sat on the top step and leaned against the porch rail. There were a lot of things he wanted to talk with Wagner about, but didn't know where to start. Cowboys weren't supposed to talk about things like love and the muddle of emotions making him dizzy. "That greenhorn, Steve, was at the entrance to the property looking to get his job back. I told him to take a hike."

"I heard about him. We don't need that kind of man on this ranch. He's lucky he's still walking after trying to mess with Jenna."

Trevor remembered the evil gleam in Steve's eyes. "He looks like trouble. I don't like it."

"Make sure the dogs are out at night for awhile."

Trevor nodded and stared down at his hands. He didn't know what to say.

"Jenna's a good woman."

Trevor looked up, surprised that Wagner knew exactly what was on his mind. "I know."

The rocker creaked as it rocked slowly back and forth. "She's been through a lot in her life and deserves to be happy. You may be like a son to me, but she's like a daughter. Are your intentions honorable?"

"Yes, sir. At first I didn't think much of it, but now—" Trevor took a breath. "I might just love her."

"Love's a big word, son. It can ruin a man just as easily as it can make life worth living." Wagner smirked, that crooked smile that could calm the most hostile man. "If you believe she's worth the effort, don't give up."

"I can't stop thinking about her." Trevor couldn't help but smile as he envisioned the blonde firecracker. Then he thought of Conner and his mood soured. "It's just so complicated."

"If you're talking about Conner, I know about him, too. Ain't much on this ranch gets by me. You should know that by now." Mr. Wagner stood, the chair continuing to rock on its own for a few moments. "Conner's one of a kind, but you know yourself, I don't keep cowboys I don't trust."

Mr. Wagner bent to clap Trevor on the shoulder before returning into the house, the screen door smacking against the frame. The dog sidled up to him and licked his cheek, but he was too lost to complain. It was time for him to man up and claim what was his before he lost it.

Chapter Twelve

Jenna spent the morning interviewing a couple laborers who stopped by for the open positions. There was some potential there, but she'd only know for sure after a few days of on-the-job training. She could usually tell if a man would last after they joined in on a cattle roundup with the regular cowboys.

The afternoon heat was barely tolerable, and sweat beaded down her cleavage. She'd love to be able to strip shirtless like the men, but was trapped in her heavy flannel. She decided to stop by the main barn to see if Trevor needed any help. The idea of seeing him again both thrilled her and sent her stomach into nervous knots. Part of her wanted to go back to the way things were, while the other part wanted to embrace their new status.

"Any luck finding help?" asked Bryce, taking her off guard.

"I have a couple interviews next week. I'll try and help out until then." She brushed past him and stopped dead when she saw Trevor bent over, cleaning his horse's hoof. As if sensing her, he glanced up and dropped the horse's leg.

"Mornin', cowboy."

He stood tall, brushing his dirty-blond hair off his forehead. "Jenna James. You have a good night?" Did she sense a note of jealousy? Men who didn't care didn't get jealous, did they?

"If you have something to say, say it." She moved in close to keep their conversation private. Cowboys were moving about everywhere.

His face lost his usual carefree quality, but looked intense and determined. Her body heated as he cornered her in the small one-horse stall. She should tell him to back off and get to work, but she wanted this, wanted him.

"It should have been you and me last night," he whispered, bracing an arm on each side of her head.

"Or maybe you should have joined us." She held eye contact with him. Desire now darkened his gaze. "I missed you." Sharing personal feelings put her at risk of getting hurt, but she had high hopes after talking with Mr. Wagner.

"Did you now?" He gave her a too-cute smirk. "Who's going to share your bed tonight, darlin'?" Jenna tamped down her urge to lash out. Trevor wasn't just any ranch hand. He was hers, and she needed to remember that. He had special leeway with her now.

"It's big enough for both of you."

He exhaled against her neck, his desire palpable. "I want you naked right here, right now. I want to suck your tits and fuck you against the wall." One of his arms dropped down and cupped her ass, pulling her tight against his erection. Knowing how good his hard cock could make her feel made her pussy weep.

"Trevor, cut it out."

"There's my name again. You know how crazy I get when you say it." He attempted to snake his hand up her shirt, but she swatted him away. Another minute and she'd succumb to his charms. It was midday, and the ranch was teeming with life. This relationship had to remain a secret, or everything she'd built over the years would crumble down around her.

She tried to switch to business mode. "You need to get to work, foreman. Anything I can do to help?"

"Yeah. I can think of a few things." Why did he have to look so damned sexy? Her body was on fire with an ache that only he could calm. It would be torture to wait so many hours before she'd get him all to herself. Before she could reply, Trevor unbuckled his thick leather belt, the silver buckle dangling to the side.

Did she dare to pleasure him? The thought of committing such a taboo act in a public place was titillating. "Someone will see," she said.

"I'll send them away. Come on, don't be cruel. Look how hard you make me."

"God help you, if anyone sees." She bent down in the corner and unzipped his jeans. His lean hips and the erotic trail of dark blond hair disappearing into his boxers made her pussy throb. She couldn't wait to wrap her lips around his cock. Being in the public place with the risk of getting caught made her randier than a cowboy.

Jenna pulled the band of his boxer briefs down to release his hard-on. He was thick and ready, his mushroom head swollen. A bead of pre-cum rolled over the rounded edge. She flicked out her tongue to tease a bit. He groaned and braced both hands on the wall. He tasted earthy and all male. She closed her eyes and wrapped her mouth around his wide girth. "You're fucking perfect," he muttered.

She gripped the base of his cock and sucked deep, working up to an eager rhythm. He was warm and silky against her tongue. When she heard boots walking up the center of the barn, she paused with his dick partway in her mouth.

"Get outta here! Can't you see I'm busy?" The harsh tone was so unlike him, but it had the desired effect. The intruders retreated, leaving them alone once again. She continued to savor his hot length until he had her head in both hands, so close to orgasm. His deep, guttural grunts encouraged her to keep going.

Then another set of footsteps broke her rhythm, a cowboy wearing spurs. This time they didn't go away when commanded, and Jenna stood up, worried about getting caught. Conner's handsome face appeared at the end of the stall. She couldn't help but replay their night together in her head, so beautifully volatile, passion and pain mixed into a memorable erotic experience.

"I've been looking for you." Conner patted the rump of the horse sharing the stall, creating a small billow of dust.

"She's with me. Where she belongs." Trevor palmed his cock, now tucked into his boxers.

Conner stood tall and unyielding at the entrance to the stall. "Who's your Big Daddy?" She swallowed hard as she glanced back and forth between both men.

Jenna leaned over and grabbed Conner's shirt, pulling him into the cramped space with her, Trevor, and the horse. "You are! Now I won't put up with a pissing contest between the two of you," she whispered harshly. "I want you both!"

They both stared at her as if flames were spewing from her mouth. She told them she wanted them—it was the truth. A dangerous truth if it wasn't reciprocated. But their male posturing gave her the hope that they reciprocated her feelings.

"I want you, too, darlin'." Trevor kissed her on the lips, but she pulled away before they got too carried away. His confession melted her heart, heating it after years of being frozen. If he was anything like her, his words carried a far deeper meaning.

She glanced up at Conner, waiting for him to say something, say anything. "You know I don't like to share."

"But you will, or I'll have your balls in a vise."

He smirked devilishly, and she knew he was on board. "You sure this is what you want?" Conner tilted her chin up. "Can I trust you with my heart?"

"You're both mine now. I'd brand you both proper if you'd let me." She tugged both of them against her, feeling overwhelmed with all the male muscle surrounding her. "Don't fuck with me or dream of hitting it with another woman. I do know how to use a rifle," she half teased.

"Only you, darlin'." Trevor trailed his lips along her jawline and whispered in her ear, "I need you."

Poor cowboy, sporting a hard-on with hours of work left in the day. She didn't want one of her men to suffer, and she'd admit her body was in a state of sweet torture with her desire to be alone with them.

"Conner, am I ready for both of you yet?" She bit her lip, knowing the suggestion would make him just as hard as Trevor. Wearing the butt plug half the night was supposed to prepare her for a double invasion.

"We can find out."

"Tack room. Now," commanded Trevor. Jenna's heart pounded in anticipation of the wicked delights in store for her. She left the stall first, walking casually to the other end of the barn to the tack room. As she walked, she scanned the area, looking for any curious onlookers, but found nothing out of the ordinary.

Inside the tack room, it was dusty and the air rich with the scent of leather. Dozens of saddles lined the windowless walls, carefully polished and preserved on saddle horses until needed. She looked around and wondered what they could use as a bed and found nothing suitable. Why would Trevor suggest the tack room? Her apartment would be the best choice, but the men were bound to be caught climbing the ladder to her loft, especially when no one was permitted but her.

The concrete floor was a mess, in need of a good sweeping. As she kicked around the mess with her boot, a heavy hand came down on her jean-clad ass. She whirled around. Conner had a hungry look in his eyes as he moved in on her. Trevor was sliding the heavy wooden door closed in the distance. Once the minimal light was choked out, she reached forward to feel for Conner. He was in the middle of taking off his shirt. She ran her hands over his chest and shoulders, loving the smooth, warm firmness of his muscled skin. God, she needed to connect. Fast.

"Who owns your cunt?" His deep baritone made her pussy spasm. She gasped with sudden need, and he hadn't even touched her yet.

"You do," she replied without thought.

Trevor struck a match and lit a lantern. He hung it up on a large nail protruding from one of the wooden wall boards and bent over to open an old restored trunk. Wagner had several of them in the house. "I think I've staked my claim on that pussy, too, darlin'. Or maybe I need to remind you."

"Take off your shirt," said Conner. The sharp lines of his face danced in the shadows of the lantern light. She wanted to feel both men touching her, kissing her, fucking her.

Once her shirt and bra were discarded, he demanded her boots be removed. She slipped them off and handed them over. When he tossed them carelessly, she snapped, "Watch it, cowboy! Wagner gave me those."

Conner unzipped his jeans. "Feisty. I think you need to be broken."

"She definitely needs taming." Trevor pulled off his shirt, leaving both men bare-chested. She needed to touch them, to lick them because looking was driving her mad with need.

Conner turned to Trevor. "I know you guys keep your treasures in that trunk. We need lube."

"That all?"

"Depends how much she wants to play," said Conner. At this point she wouldn't say no to much. She trusted them not to hurt her, which was half the battle. These men had opened Pandora's box and released the sensual woman that had been dormant and ashamed of her sexuality all these years.

"Do you wanna play, darlin'?" Trevor was still too far away for her liking, over by the open trunk. "How'd you like a dildo inside your sweet little pussy?"

She nodded, feeling empty and ready for her men and their games. Trevor grabbed some things from the trunk and sauntered over to her with a look of satisfaction glued on his face. He coated a flesh-colored dildo with lubricant and held it in front of her for her inspection. It was nearly as large as the real deal. The toy waggled around tauntingly in front of her. She shucked her pants and eagerly awaited their next move.

"Lie down on the bench, Jenna." She complied, lowering her nude form onto the wooden bleacher-style bench. As much as she wanted this, she couldn't help but think of all the other women they must have brought to this same room.

Trevor knelt beside her and parted her legs with one hand, while guiding the slick phallus into her cunt. It was cold, not comforting and hot like his cock, but it filled her and dulled her need temporarily. She wrapped an arm around his neck and pulled him close. He pumped the silicone dick in and out of her body while she whispered in his ear. "How am I any different from all your other women?"

He frowned, and stilled his movements. "Don't you know? Jenna, it's always been you. I love you, and now that I have you, there'll never be anyone else."

She liked the sound of that—it was everything she wanted to hear. With a deep inhale to chase away her remaining doubts, she arched up to receive more of the dildo. He rewarded her by fucking her with the toy and teasing her clit with his free hand. This was crazy, dirty sex, and she loved every second of it.

* * * *

Trevor leaned in and sucked her clit until she squealed for him to stop. He didn't know how much longer he could hold off. Jenna's beautiful naked body was laid out before him like a banquet, and he wanted to sample every part of her.

"She can't handle having her pussy sucked?" Conner removed his pants and sat on the bench behind her head. "That's pathetic and deserves punishment."

"Conner," Trevor warned.

"Didn't she tell you that she loves to get spanked?" Conner helped her sit up, and then stand. Although Trevor wasn't into kink like Conner, the idea piqued his interest.

When Conner patted his lap, his cock jutting out from between his legs, Jenna didn't hesitate to lie over his thighs, her ripe, round ass kissing the open air. He began to rub her flesh in firm circles, and Jenna ground her pussy against his leg in response.

Whack!

Trevor half expected Jenna to let loose a string of curses, but she only moaned in pleasure, wiggling her ass for more. *Whack! Whack! Whack!* Even in the dim lighting, Trevor could see her milky white ass turning a pretty pink. Conner twisted and lay over the bench, pulling Jenna atop him as he shifted. Now straddling his waist, she rose up on her feet and pulled the dildo free, dropping it to the ground. Then she impaled herself over Conner's ready cock.

Trevor always loved bringing women back to the tack room, especially the ones that didn't mind sharing their body with a group of cowboys. The more, the merrier, in his opinion. But as he watched Jenna ride Conner, her full breasts bouncing temptingly, he realized he'd never be able to share her with other men from the crew. He also became aware that he wasn't just in this for cheap thrills. He wanted more than sex, more than a few nights of pleasure from Jenna. Wagner was right—it was love. It burned inside him and left no doubt in his heart.

Now it was time to make their triad official. Just Jenna, Conner, and Trevor. He lubed up his cock and straddled the bench behind Jenna. He pushed her down against Conner with a palm to her back and positioned his dick at her tight rosette. Trevor had deflowered too many women to remember, but nothing could compare to this. He pressed the head of his cock inside her using firm, consistent pressure.

"Remember the butt plug? Just push against him and relax," said Conner, who now began to kiss Jenna. She whined and grunted in discomfort as he worked his way into her tight nether hole. Once fully seated, he took a much-needed cleansing breath and allowed her time to adjust to his cock filling her ass. Damn, she was tight.

"How does it feel to have my dick in your ass?" He gripped her hips, squeezing the soft flesh as he waited like a horse at the starting gates.

She said nothing, but her breathing changed from rapid to controlled, and he knew it was only a matter of minutes until her body accepted him. He reached between her body and Conner's to play with her clit. The added stimulation would put her over the edge, allow her to relax and enjoy what they planned to give her.

"Both our cocks are inside you, Jenna. Be a good girl and tell me how that feels." Conner hadn't thrust once since Trevor joined them, maintaining herculean control considering the temptation sitting on his cock.

"Tight. Full."

"Do you want us to double fuck you now?"

She nodded, and they began to work her, slowly and rhythmically, until she was grinding against them and begging for more. They took turns, working together, double-teaming. Trevor and Conner seemed to work like a well-oiled machine, as if they were meant to have Jenna sandwiched between them. He could feel the other man's cock sliding against his, only a thin membrane between them.

Nothing could compare to sharing a woman, especially when love was involved. Trevor held no animosity for Conner. Their ménage felt natural and right.

"You're fucking tight, darlin'. I love it." Trevor was too close to the edge. He needed Jenna to finish before him, so held off. Feeling her ass clamp around him, her body so stuffed with cock, had his sanity hanging on by a thread.

"Oh, God, it's happening," she cried. "Everything's getting warm. It's building inside me—"

"Let loose, sweetheart. Embrace it. Focus on that pleasure point inside you and let it take over." Trevor helped her along by pulling at her clit, giving her that extra push over the edge. It worked—her body clamped down around his cock, and he could feel wave after wave milking him. Conner groaned and pulled her down to his chest. Trevor finally allowed himself to come, filling her ass full of seed. He groaned, and then smoothed his hands over her sweat-slick back as he took a cleansing breath.

"Oh, my God, that felt good," she said. Trevor gently slipped out of her ass and rummaged around for his shirt. He'd need to get a quick shower in before returning to work. He had a shipment of cattle to drive out to the other end of town before dinner hour.

Once dressed, Trevor leaned over. Jenna was still lying on top of Conner's chest, completely spent. "I'll see you tonight, darlin'." He kissed her sweat-slick forehead before standing. "Take care of her," he told Conner.

Chapter Thirteen

Over a week had passed since the afternoon foray in the tack room. Jenna snuck out to Conner's cabin most nights, where he'd be waiting for her with Trevor. It wasn't always about the sex. Some nights they just slept together, but it felt good not to be alone anymore. Everything was just too good to be true. But good things didn't last. How long could they meet up like this? How long could they hide their threesome without one of the other cowboys getting wise? Jenna couldn't even think of the next logical step to take because the entire relationship was so unorthodox. The Wagner Ranch was her home. She wasn't the housewife type—Jenna was a cowgirl right down to her marrow and could never fulfill a typical role as wife or mother.

The second breakfast run was in full swing. She helped Pete serve and maintain order. Trevor and Conner both sat at the table, glancing at her with sexy grins. She only scowled, scared they'd give away their hidden relationship.

Jenna slipped into the main house when things settled down. Grace and Scott had returned home the night before from their honeymoon. Scott was busy moving their stuff to their newly renovated home a few miles away. Mr. Wagner parceled off a breathtaking piece of land for them to build on. There was a river running through it, fertile land, and a mix of fields and forest. The perfect place to settle down and raise a family.

She knocked softly on Grace's bedroom door. "Come in."

Jenna slipped in and closed the door behind her. "Did I wake you?"

Grace shook her head and sat up in the bed, her long, dark hair falling over her shoulders. "How were things while we were gone?"

Jenna almost choked on laughter. What hadn't happened? "Real good. I'm glad you're back safe and sound, though." She sat on the edge of the bed. Grace was her only female friend, but she also didn't know the truth about Jenna. "Can I ask you somethin'?"

"Of course."

"I know you were worried about Scott wanting you when you first came here. You felt unworthy because of the things you did on the ranch." Grace's face turned a shade of pink, but everyone knew what she'd done with the cowboys. "How did you get over it?"

She reflected for a moment. "I decided it didn't matter what other people thought. What mattered was my happiness. If Scott and I loved each other, then nobody else should be able to stand in our way."

That's exactly what she expected Grace to say, and the precise advice she needed. Unfortunately, Jenna was a coward. Too afraid to embrace the life she wanted due to unsubstantiated fears. She knew Trevor and Conner loved her, but unlearning years of holding back her emotions and putting on a façade wasn't easy. The worst part was knowing she had to come clean, to tell her men the ugly truth about her past. Would they still love her? In her heart, she knew the truth was the real barrier keeping her from committing.

Jenna decided she had to woman up and tell them the truth. She'd come close a couple times during the past week, but chickened out. After breakfast, the guys would get back to work, so she planned to meet them in the barn and pull them aside before she lost her nerve.

She left Grace to dress for breakfast and head to the barn. Before turning the corner, hidden by a stall divider, she heard the greenhorn, Steve's, voice. Her jaw immediately clenched down hard as her anger rose to dangerous levels. He had the nerve to show up at the ranch again? In the light of day she'd be able to deal with him good and proper.

"I knew I'd heard that name before—Jenna James. She's trouble. She gave the cops a false report about her neighbor assaulting her and nearly ruined his life. It was in all the papers a few years back. I'm surprised you didn't hear. Jenna's an attention-seeker and a troublemaker."

She should grab her rifle from her apartment above her and teach that no-gooder some manners. But he knew about her, her real life, her secrets. He was in her territory, spreading rumors—why? Just to get revenge because he lost a minimum wage job? The information he offered would certainly destroy her. Was her life worth only that much? She didn't want Trevor and Conner to find out about her past like this, tainted by lies. Jenna didn't need pity, nor did she need to be looked at with disgust—not from the two men she loved. She didn't hear their voices, so if she dealt with Steve quickly, maybe that would be the end of it. But what if the other hired hands spread word? Of course they would.

"That doesn't sound like Jenna," said Bryce.

She tried to calm her breathing before facing off with that yellow belly. Then she heard his voice. "What's going on here? I thought I told you you weren't welcome around here." Trevor's commanding voice surpassed the others.

"I'm just doing a service, telling these men about the real woman they work with."

"What are you blathering about?"

"Jenna tried to send an innocent man to prison, lying about being raped. She's sick and spiteful."

"Mind your tongue, Steve. We don't take well to strangers bad-mouthing our crew."

"Maybe next time she'll report one of you if you get on her bad side. They'll believe her because she's a woman."

Jenna may be strong, but right now she felt smaller than an ant. Then she noticed Conner standing behind the crowd. He'd heard every word, too. She lost her bravery and retreated further into the barn.

"You little fuck." Trevor bolted forward and grabbed Steve by the scruff of the shirt and slammed him against the side of the barn. None of the other half dozen cowboys made a move to help the greenhorn. "Nothing you can say will tarnish Jenna's image, only serve to piss us off."

"What the fuck are you all looking at? Get to work!" Conner roared.

Once at the other end of the barn, she untethered her horse, mounted, and rode. She didn't know where she was going, or what she'd do when she and the horse tired, but she had to escape. Escape the truth, escape reality.

When she was far from the barn, she slipped off her horse, twirling around in the beautiful open fields with her arms splayed as she stared up at the sky. She felt like a madwoman, ready to break.

* * * *

Conner saw Jenna's horse make like a bat out of hell in the distance. She must have heard everything. He told Trevor to take care of Steve once and for all, and then meet them at his cabin.

He slowed his horse as he neared Jenna's location. Her gelding grazed off in the near distance, and she sat cross-legged in the long grass. No tears stained her face, but she looked broken. His heart went out to her.

"No more secrets, little one." He wasn't going to bullshit her with sweet words and kisses. This was Jenna.

"You already know. If they could lock him up for the rest of his life, it wouldn't be enough to make up for what he did to me. I came here to escape the past. Yeah, I lied about some things, but I never backstabbed anyone. I work just as hard as everyone else on this ranch." Her eyes appeared red-rimmed. She shouldn't have to defend herself because she was the victim. "My father's best friend stole my innocence. That's not my fault!" Her anger melted around her after admitting the truth out loud.

"I'd never blame you." Conner lifted her up and helped her mount his horse before climbing on behind her. Her gelding would return to the ranch on its own.

"Don't let them see me cry," she repeated as they neared the ranch.

Once inside his cabin, he gripped her shoulders and sat her on the bed. He knelt down in front of her and took her hands in his. Conner wanted to confess his undying love for her. He needed her to know that nothing could tarnish her image in his eyes, but nothing came out of his mouth. Everything was said through their touch and eye contact.

The door burst open, and Trevor plucked his cowboy hat off as he tried to catch his breath. "You all right, darlin'? I came as fast as I could."

"Do you think less of me?" she whispered.

"Why would I think less of you?" Trevor dropped down beside Conner. "You're the bravest, most beautiful woman I've ever met, and nothing will ever change that."

"Everything's in the open now, so no more hiding," said Conner. "You're ours, and I want the world to know it."

"Don't you two get it? How will I get respect from the men now? I know all about cowboys, and they won't leave me alone. I don't think Wagner would appreciate it if I shot all his staff because that's what I'll end up doing."

Conner and Trevor stood and laughed at the same unspoken joke. Jenna scowled. "What's funny?"

Trevor answered, "Darlin', I'm the ranch foreman, and Conner's the most bad-ass cowboy on the crew. The men wouldn't dare give you a sideways glance now that you're ours."

* * * *

Jenna insisted she had to spill the news to Wagner first thing. So after dinner, Conner followed Trevor and Jenna into the main living room of the house. Mr. Wagner was sitting by the crackling fire, drinking a cup of hot chocolate with Ms. Scarlett. Trevor had strong ties with the older man, but through only a fault of his own Conner had less of a bond. He kept to himself, letting his hatred eat him from the inside out. Not anymore. Jenna had been through even worse than he had, and she was a survivor. He refused to dwell on a past he couldn't undo.

"Howdy, Wagner," Trevor greeted, leaning an elbow on the fireplace mantle. Conner stood at the end of the couch, while Jenna dropped down beside Mr. Wagner and accepted a hug.

"What do I owe the pleasure?"

Conner usually remained silent, but not today. "We're moving out, the three of us."

"What?" Jenna bolted to attention. "Conner—"

Mr. Wagner held no worry in his eyes hearing that his three best workers would be leaving. He only smiled softly, his movements slow as he patted each woman on the leg on either side of him. "Do you think that's a wise decision, Conner? Seems the challenge in this relationship is living accommodations, am I right?"

"Yes, sir."

He turned to Jenna. "Well, since my best girl has decided to settle down with two of my best cowboys, I think I should offer an early wedding gift." Jenna twisted and held Mr. Wagner's flannel sleeve like an excited schoolgirl. "That's right. You choose your piece of land, Jenna, and it's yours. You put these two boys to work building you a place of your own."

Chapter Fourteen

"It's perfect. I love it." Jenna spun around to take in all the scenery. The forest to the north provided privacy and a place to hike or ride the trails. The fields were rolling and already planted with barley.

"Then it's settled then," said Mr. Wagner. He signed the papers the lawyer laid on the hood of the truck, and just like that, they had their own land.

She waved good-bye as Mr. Wagner drove off with the lawyer. It was only a few minutes' drive to the ranch.

"You see how fast he barreled out of here," said Trevor, cupping a hand over his eyes to see down the road.

"He's just anxious to get back to his lady. I've never seen him so in love." Jenna couldn't be happier that Mr. Wagner and Ms. Scarlett had hit it off. She was a nice lady, and thankfully her wild children had already returned home and were out of Jenna's hair.

"I know how he feels," said Trevor, pulling her against him. "I wish our place was already built because I'd love to christen our bedroom."

She kissed his stubbly chin and proceeded to pace the area they planned to build on. "So tell me, where would the bedroom be? At the back, facing the forest, or up front closer to the road?" She could already envision it. It would be simple, functional, built by her men. But it would be home, and it would house good memories.

"Let's play house. Right now," said Trevor, grabbing her from behind, making her squeal.

"Mansfield, don't tell me you'd actually fuck me right here, right now. Have you no shame?"

"Not when it comes to you." With his arms snaked around her, he began unbuttoning her jeans. Her body heated just thinking about the future with her two cowboys.

Conner came around in front of her. He pulled her shirt up over her head and unclasped her bra. She scanned the area to ensure their privacy, but only found open fields, the wind like a wave through the barley. "You're going along with this?" she asked Conner.

"Behave, Jenna. Your Big Daddy wants a taste of your pussy."

"You're a cowgirl. You afraid of getting a little dirty?" Trevor pulled her jeans down her hips.

Her men were driving her wild. Their hands were everywhere, and their voices carried such a deep, sexy drawl. Conner dropped down and kissed her clit once before continuing down to lie on his back. His clothes were still on, but he unbuttoned his checkered shirt, exposing his ripped torso, and unzipped his jeans to release his monster cock, fully erect and tempting. The sight of him laying there was all the invitation she needed.

Trevor released her, and she moved like a magnet toward Conner, stepping out of her jeans and straddling his waist. She wasted no time in sinking over his hot length. His cock filled her, warmed her, and chased away that erotic itch that erupted in her every time they toyed with her.

"I can't wait to start working on our house," said Trevor. He bent over and kissed her lips while she fucked the man beneath her, riding him hard the way he liked it. She watched Trevor walk around the area, mentally planning his building strategy. The men were so comfortable with sharing her, it continued to amaze her how perfect the three of them were together. When she couldn't have both, they ensured at least one of them was looking out for her, a team of overprotective lovers, soon-to-be husbands. It warmed her heart, especially when she needed no saving. She'd used her shotgun since their relationship was made public, scaring some manners into one of the farmhands when he gave her lip. Everything outside of their relationship managed to stay the same, eliminating all her worries about coming out.

"Trevor!"

"Darlin'?" He returned to her and bent down on one knee. Trevor stilled her movements with a hand around her small ribs, before leaning down to suck her pert nipple.

"You can plan the house later. Right now, I need you to join us." An orgasm while filled with two cocks was immeasurably more satisfying, and she was close to coming.

"Yes, ma'am." He danced out of his boots and lost his pants before kneeling back behind her. His rough hands smoothed down her bare back, sending shivers skittering along her skin. Then he smacked her ass with a strong cowboy hand. "Bend over, darlin'." She collapsed against Conner's hard chest, accepting the kisses he offered.

Trevor used his own saliva to moisten her ass as he penetrated her with two moist fingers. She clenched around Conner's dick, making him groan and grab her hips. When Trevor eased his cock into her tight ass, she hissed as she took inch after inch of his steely erection. He fought for room inside her as his dick collided with Conner's, only a thin membrane separating them. She knew her cowboys loved the intensity of double-teaming her, both their cocks snuggly filling her, enhancing their enjoyment.

"Tell Trevor you love it when he fucks you up the ass," said Conner, looking up at her with hooded eyes.

"Yes!" They both pumped into her like a perfectly synched fucking machine, driving her mad with desire. The open air caressed her bare skin, and she was soon lost to the moment as her orgasm began to rise. "I'm so close. Don't stop!"

She heard the distant rumble of the earth, signaling a truck was coming down the abandoned dirt road. Right now all that mattered was reaching her peak. The idea of being caught in the open in their predicament made her pussy more desperate. It was right there on the surface, taunting her, waiting to be freed. When Trevor's hand came around and pinched her nipple, she lost it. Her body detonated and claimed both cocks, pulling them deeper and setting off a ripple effect of orgasms.

"Who the fuck would dare come way out here?" Conner grated as they separated and pulled on their clothes.

Jenna walked to the side of the road and grabbed her rifle out of the truck bed, leaning it against her shoulder.

When the other truck arrived, Bryce and Seth slammed their doors behind them as they rushed over. "Trouble," said Bryce.

Conner and Trevor were both back on the ground, absorbing the warm rays of sunshine on the spot that would soon be their family home, both spent from lovemaking.

"What now?" asked Trevor, no hint of worry in his tone.

"Cattle thieves on the west end. What should we do?" It was still a working day. They'd only come out to finalize the land transfer with Wagner and the lawyer. Sometimes she thought the cowboys couldn't think without their foreman dolling out the orders.

Cattle rustlers were nothing new on a billion-dollar cattle farm. The property was vast, and they couldn't be everywhere all the time. But Jenna didn't take kindly to anyone trying to rip off Wagner. She glanced over at her lazy lovers. They looked to each other with a grin and then answered in unison. "Jenna'll handle them."

THE END

WWW.STACEYESPINO.COM

ABOUT THE AUTHOR

Stacey Espino resides in beautiful Ontario, Canada where she is busy raising her five school-aged children. She loves being a Canadian, but could do without the brutal winters. When she's not escaping into the romantic settings she creates on her laptop, she's reading one of the many books threatening to overtake her bedroom. With a passion for the paranormal, she wrote *Fearless Desires*, the first Siren-Bookstrand novel in her Immortal Love series.

Also by Stacey Espino

Siren Classic: Immortal Love 1: *Fearless Desires*
Siren Classic: Immortal Love 2: *Fearless Love*
Ménage and More: *Saving Grace*
Ménage Amour: *Damaged Cowboys*
Ménage Amour: Love Bites 1: *Two Wolves Are Better Than One*
Ménage Amour: Love Bites 2: *Bella's Wolves*
Siren Classic: Forbidden Attraction: *Womankind*
Ménage Amour: *Cowboy Domination*

Available at
BOOKSTRAND.COM

Siren Publishing, Inc.
www.SirenPublishing.com

CPSIA information can be obtained at www.ICGtesting.com
231134LV00008B/233/P

9 781610 346429